SOCIAL SECURITY

A Novel for Our Time

Arlene E. Smith

For Matthew

Who never got to grow old

FOREWORD

SOCIAL SECURITY is the story of college friends in the 60's who somehow manage to find each other again when they are in their 60's. I had no shortage of material, being a part of the same era.

As I've worked on this project and shared the story, family and friends have asked if they are included within its pages. I tell them that all characters in the book are fictional and don't represent any one individual, however they are, indeed, all in the book. In other words, we are all in it.

I've grabbed bits and pieces of my past and my present. I've also shamelessly stolen thoughts and lines from my current social groups at the Nut House Brewery, the Black Rock Café and my local VFW. In addition, my geographic and event narrative is not up for fact checking, but instead, adapted for general context.

As noted American author and college professor, Joseph Campbell once said: "Our life evokes our character and you find out more about yourself as you go on."

That's what I hope this book does for all of you.

Regardless of your age or generation, I invite you to explore the world of SOCIAL SECURITY. Rest assured, you're all in there...

CHAPTER ONE

"**M**y life is over!" he sobbed as his legs buckled and he dropped to the sidewalk, the opened envelope still clutched tightly in his hand. Ezekiel Merriweather Martin sat in a puddle next to the mailbox kiosk near his Portland houseboat. Other 'liveaboards' nearby knew him well and just sighed a little as they stepped around him to check for their own mail. Still sobbing, Ezekiel looked out toward the beautiful river under clear blue skies and cried out again, "My life is over! Why me? Why me?"

"Ziggy? Is that you, man?"

Was that God? Ezekiel figured he had to be hearing God's voice calling him home. Well that's OK, he was ready. Hadn't he just said his life was over? Geez, the Lord had taken him seriously. Kind of a bummer now that he was dead to find out he had a direct line to God.

"Ziggy? Ziggy Martin? Is that you?"

Ezekiel looked up through watery eyes. Hardly anyone had called him Ziggy in more than 40 years…. no one still alive, at least. Yeah, he thought, I must be dead. Someone up there is calling me. But no, he was still sitting on the sidewalk, still clutching the envelope, and staring up into a face that showed as many years as his, but had a familiar feel about it. OK, he thought… Add a beard and some hair on top and you've got….

"Al?" he croaked. "Al Smith? Ouch!" He guessed he wasn't dead because as he tried to stand up, he stuck his hand on a piece of glass.

"You OK, Ziggy?" asked Al, trying to help him up without falling down himself.

1

"Oh, yeah, I guess so," said Ziggy. "Thought I was dead, and then figured you were dead and we were both dead and in heaven, but I guess we're still here, right?"

"Damn right," agreed Al and they both started laughing.

"So, what are you doing here, Al?" Ziggy asked. "I thought you were up in Seattle with your kids and grandkids."

"Yeah, I was," said Al, "But things got sort of uncomfortable."

"Got caught smoking pot in the garage again?" asked Ziggy.

"Yeah, and then there was this lady friend I had and she kept calling and coming over all times of day and night. I just needed my space… space away from her and the kids and the grandkids. We're all good. I just thought I'd head south and see what Portland has to offer. Never thought I'd run into you down here. Thought you were in San Francisco."

Al was trying to dust Ziggy off and Ziggy was still trying to figure out what was going on. It had been years since Ziggy had heard from Al, and even longer since he'd seen him. He'd gotten older, but then Ziggy knew he had too. But Al still had the sparkle in his eyes and good-natured grin on his face.

"Nah, too crowded and way too expensive," Ziggy said. "Portland is pretty pricey too, but I found myself a great deal on a place down here and I've been calling it home for the past three years or so." Ziggy saw no need to further explain his move from San Diego to San Francisco to retirement in Portland. "Hey Al, now that we're not dead, we could get out of the way here and head down to my boat and visit some more. It's great seeing you… We can just talk over a couple of brews."

"No," Al said. "Can't do that. Had to give that stuff up. My liver and all just sort of told me it was time to call it quits on alcohol. Actually, the doctor was the one that talked to my liver and then relayed the message to me. But I could smoke a joint with ya…not completely vice-free, you know?"

"Sounds good," agreed Ziggy. He kind of liked thinking of himself as Ziggy again. It made him feel younger. He led Al down the steep narrow gangplank to his dock and toward the middle of the float to his boat, 'Delilah'. "Not big, not pretty, but it's home and it suits me fine," Ziggy explained as they stepped aboard. "There's plenty of fancier floating homes around here, but that's not my style anyway, even if I could afford one."

"So, is this a houseboat or a floating home or what?" asked Al.

"Technically, it's a floating home because it has no motor. A houseboat has to have a motor," said Ziggy as he started shuffling in a drawer in the kitchen. "But floating home sounds too grand for this place, so I call everything a houseboat except for the really fancy ones. He finally came up with a small baggie and some rolling papers. As he started rolling a joint, Al looked around, although there wasn't a whole lot to look at. A decent size living area with a small kitchenette tucked away in the corner; down a short hall to a bedroom and very small bathroom that not only held the necessities, but also an ancient stacked washer and dryer.

"Well, it looks like you've got everything you need, man," said Al. "I definitely approve."

"Have a seat," said Ziggy as he lit and inhaled before he passed the joint to his long lost (but not dead) pal. "We've got lots of catching up to do."

Al took a dedicated drag, leaned back in the only easy chair in the place, and smiled.

"Oh yeah, this is good. Gotta say though, I think it all seemed better when it wasn't legal you know. Sort of takes some of the rush out of it. But still good Zig, still good." As Al continued to relax, he asked Ziggy,

"Say, you seemed to keep up with the old gang more than I did. How is everyone doing these days?"

"Oh, I don't know," Ziggy said, trying to hold in the smoke and talk at the same time. "We all got into our jobs, careers, families, and it's gotten harder to keep up anymore. Boy, we hung out with a fun group back then. I remember most all of them still."

"Yeah," agreed Al. "So, what about Zola? She was a foxy one for sure."

"Dead," Ziggy replied.

"Zola? Dead? How?"

"Heart attack. Right in the middle of her 60th birthday celebration, had to be four or five years ago. Not sure if she got into the cake and champagne before it happened."

"Wow, Zola, gone," said Al, shaking his head. "And what was his name? The guy that she hung around with for a while, Frank?"

"Dead," Ziggy replied, letting the joint burn out in the ashtray.

"Frank? Dead? How?"

"I'm thinking it was work-related," Ziggy said thoughtfully. "He moved to the Seattle area and took over his dad's business. I think he was into heavy equipment and all and it happened on the job. I sent a sympathy card, but that was a while ago. Come to think of it, everything seems to have happened a while ago." Ziggy closed his eyes to think. He did some of his best thinking with his eyes closed (unless he fell asleep).

"Boy, Frank too. Well, I certainly remember Ryan. Now I wouldn't be surprised to hear he was into something pretty exciting. Always lived on the edge. How's old Ryan doing Zig? asked Al."

"Dead," Ziggy said and added, "mountain climbing" before Al could ask how.

"Ryan gone. Boy that sounds like the way he would have wanted to go, though. Good old Ryan."

"OK... Ned?" asked Al. "Ned was a little younger than us as I recall, a real go-getter too. He was one of the best protestors we had. I remember the grand plans he believed in, for himself and for our country, too. How the heck is Ned?"

"Underground," Ziggy replied, still with his eyes closed.

"Ned is dead too?" shouted Al. "How?"

Ziggy opened his eyes with a start. "Ned's not dead, he's underground, in Canada. Remember when he thought he was going to be drafted? Used up all his deferments and saw the writing on the wall. So, he went underground...guess it must be 30 years since I heard from him. He was in Canada then and still making grand plans, just for another country."

"Yeah that was our Ned, grand plans." Then Al quickly changed the subject. "You know, Ziggy, I'm getting kind of hungry. I noticed there was a lunch wagon across the street at that shipyard. Want to join me for a hot dog or something? My treat."

"Sure," Ziggy said. He was marveling at what was happening. It got him thinking about those days at the University of California at San Francisco. "Just let me get myself together."

When Ziggy was ready, they both headed back up the gangplank to venture across the road to the smallish marine facility.

"No crosswalks, huh?" asked Al.

"Nope," said Ziggy. "We just take our chances."

"Yeah, well that's the way to live, I guess," said Al.

"Yeah, except for Ryan," Ziggy sighed.

"Oh, yeah, Ryan," agreed Al, as he carefully looked both ways.

After Ziggy and Al got their lunch from the wagon, they sat at one of the picnic benches in the shade of a great old cedar tree. "These food trucks are great," said Al, as he started in on his taco. "They seem to be all over Portland. You know I really like the vibe around here. Wish I could find an affordable place to live in this area, but so far, everything is way out of my price range."

"You're right, Al," said Ziggy. "Those are pricey condos over there, but a hell of a view. And over there," Ziggy pointed to more condos. "And then there's the City of Portland," and he pointed to the sprawling metropolis. "It's all expensive."

"And then there's the water," agreed Al, looking at the beautiful river while taking another bite of his taco. "I was really hoping I could find a place of my own down here, but not much in the way of options."

"Well, maybe there is an option," said Ziggy thoughtfully (for which he had to close his eyes again). "Let me think on that a bit. Not to change the subject, but what were you doing around here anyway?" Ziggy asked.

"Looking for a part time job," Al said. "My savings are running low and my tiny pension and Social Security just aren't going to cut it."

"Oh yeah, Social Security," Ziggy said, as he remembered the letter in the envelope at home. "And I find out today that we get no cost of living increase in Social Security next year. I was sort of counting on that," he added, tearing up again.

"Is that what got you on the ground moaning about when I found you?" asked Al.

"Yeah," Ziggy said. "I'm not usually so dramatic, as you know, but that notice was just too much for me today. I'm OK with what I'm getting, got a few investments, but that houseboat doesn't maintain itself and it's probably as old as we are. I've been lucky so far, but since I know nothing about boats, anything that comes up, I pretty much have to pay to get it worked on."

Al's eyes lifted from his meal and said, "Well, I have a ton of experience with boats. Worked on them in California and kind of hung around the marinas in Seattle and got odd jobs when I could. That's why I was looking for a job here," he said, gesturing to the boat yard behind them. "But the only thing they have right now that they would agree to hire me for is a part time night watchman and I can't do that."

"Why not?" asked Ziggy, finishing up his lemonade with a slurp.

"Well, I have no wheels, and the buses or MAX don't run the hours I would need to work," said Al. "Never mind the fact that I have no place I can afford to live. I can't stay in a motel forever. Another dead end I guess. Sure do like it here though."

"Well, here's an idea," said Ziggy as he slammed his hand on the table. "Ouch," he added as he realized that was the same hand he'd cut on the glass when he thought he was dead. "There's a guy a couple of boats down from me that wants to sell his place. It's in pretty rough shape and so is the guy; his kids are going to take him in. You said you have savings left?"

"Well, yeah," Al said slowly. "But not a lot. I get my pension and my Social Security — with no cost of living increase — I guess, but I don't have much for a down payment. And if it needs work..." he left that thought hanging.

"No problem," said Ziggy, all excited. "As long as you can show you can make the monthly payments and moorage rent, I'm sure you could work something out. But I told you it needs a lot of work."

"Well, hell, I don't mind work," Al said. "And if I lived right across the street, I could pick up some hours as night watchman here. And I could help you with your repairs as you need them. So you won't have to drop to the sidewalk again any time soon," he added with a laugh.

"Look," Ziggy said. "I'll talk to the guy tonight when he gets back from visiting his kids. They'll bring him home, so they'd be around too. You come by tomorrow and we'll take a look and see what you think of it and what they think of you. And then you can high tail it to the personnel office over there and take that part time job. This could be the best day that ever happened to us."

"Yeah," Al agreed. "Although we've had some pretty good days, remember?"

"Oh yeah," said Ziggy, eyes closed again. "I remember."

CHAPTER TWO

Peter Sullivan was an asshole. I suppose in our dream world back then, where everyone was supposed to love one another and just get along that is the wrong thing to say. But I said it then and I'll say it now. Peter Sullivan was an asshole. He was arrogant, pushy, cruel at times, dishonest and more. Everyone knew it. Peter Sullivan knew it. I am sure he cultivated it to the fine art that was him — proud of it in a way. But Peter Sullivan III had one great quality. He was a rich boy.

Gotta give Peter his due, though. If it hadn't been for him, the bunch of us would probably never have gotten together back then. Not that we sought him out as the rich kid, but rather he sought our little group out. Not because he wanted to be in our crowd. Heavens no. Not because he envied us. God forbid. But because we had something that he wanted: Marcia Gideon.

Marcia Gideon was a sophomore like a lot of us. She transferred from a junior college down south somewhere. Every campus has a Marcia Gideon type. Marcia was smart. She was friendly. She was funny. And she was drop dead gorgeous — by far the most beautiful girl on campus. And Peter Sullivan wanted the best.

Although our group grew in size over that sophomore year, we started out with only five of us: me, Al, Ryan, Paula and Zola. People drifted in and out, but that was our core. Then Marcia stopped by our lunch table on the lawn and our group started to grow. Everyone wanted to hang out with Marcia and thus, with us. So when Peter Sullivan approached me one day, I was not really surprised. He had made a name for himself already. Besides being *an asshole, he was pretty smart, a leader, a wise cracker when he wanted to be, and of course, rich.*

"Hey Zeke," (I was Zeke back then) he said as we were packing up our books at the end of our applied mathematics class.

I smiled and said, "Hey," figuring that was going to be it. But not that time…

"I just rented this huge house over in Oakland and was thinking of throwing a party to christen the place. What do you say you and your crowd come on over next Saturday? There'll be lots of booze and other stuff, if you know what I mean. And the place has so much room you all could just hang out until Sunday if you feel like it. What do you say?" I closed my eyes to think about that out-of-left-field offer. Peter must have thought I was making some kind of statement and asked what the heck I was doing. I was a little embarrassed to tell this New York hotshot how I usually processed things.

"Oh, I'm just thinking," I replied. "Your invite sounds OK to me. I'll ask some of the guys if they want to party next Saturday."

"And some of the girls, too?" Peter asked with a smile.

Oh sure, that was it. We were welcome as long as we brought him a housewarming gift… Marcia Gideon.

The party was great. I mean it was really perfect — a break in the Bay area weather, a nice warm pool, plenty of stuff to make you mellow and a really good group of people. I knew a lot of them, but there were some from other schools and stuff. But by the end of the evening, we had all gotten to know one another pretty well and we were all cool with each other. Especially Zola and Frank.

Frank was a junior at Berkeley and a real smooth operator. I mean, he could really play the guitar instead of just fooling around and strumming like most of us did back then. Zola was entranced. I think we all were. He seemed like a nice guy, but a lot of us felt pretty protective of Zola. Zola was quite good looking and was a lot of fun, but sometimes she got a little carried away with her drama. I guess that made some sense, since she had declared herself as a drama major. She'd fallen for jerks in the past, and we tried to keep an eye on her. But Frank was a good guy as far as we could tell, so it all seemed fine.

Peter Sullivan was more than fine. Marcia had warmed right up to him and I have to admit they made a pretty good couple. I'm sure hundreds of hearts were probably broken around campus as they appeared to be headed for couple-dom. But we were all so young back then - just living for the moment - so no one really knew where couples that night would end up the next day or the next week or the next month. At that point, we weren't thinking of anything further into the future than that.

I hung around with Al for a while, but soon he was off with some of the girls he found. Al had always been in love with women and he fell in and out of love at pretty consistent intervals. No harm, no foul, was Al's motto, and many of his 'girls' remained good friends.

Ryan was in the pool a good deal of the night. Tall and blond, he was always the athletic and daring one. He was at home in the water; whether on skis, in a boat, or just swimming laps. He liked to snow ski and had talked about sky diving some time when he could afford it. He wanted to be a high school teacher and he thought he'd probably coach some sport as well. Ryan was like that. He wasn't what you'd call a 'jock,' but more just into the thrill of the action. He and I got along well, even though my interest in any sport activity was limited to a beer in my hand and my butt on the couch in front of the television.

I got involved in a few conversations, but pretty much hung around with Paula. We had been in lust for a while, but decided that being friends would last longer and suited us better. It was a good mix of people and Peter's place was really awesome.

"So, what do you think about all this?" Paula asked me as we went to the bar to get a couple more Tequila Sunrises. "I mean, this is great, but is it really us?" We sat down in nearby beanbag chairs and studied the crowd.

"I think it's us, it could be us," I said as I closed my eyes and thought about it. "I mean we're here aren't we, and we're enjoying ourselves and the others here, aren't we? So, yeah, it's maybe an evolution of us."

Paula was cool. She was a psychology major so she, of course, had to practice on all of us. That was fine most of the time, although I always thought it might be better if she was a massage therapist major (That was an honest to God course at one of the community colleges). She had dark hair, was a little plump, but mostly in good places, and we got along great. We met on the first day of our freshman year and after the brief romance, we'd been best friends ever since. We'd both had unusual childhoods, so we were able to understand many of each other's quirks. I knew she'd had to put off college for a year to work and earn enough money to supplement her student loans and grants. She worked part time at the university bookstore while carrying a full load of credits.

"Yeah, you might be right, Zeke," she agreed. "We all need to evolve, or rather we should evolve. This could be our evolution revolution," she said and poked at me to open my eyes so we could laugh together at that one.

The night went on and the hits kept coming. By the wee hours, the crowd was thinning. Some had gone home while they could still find home. Our gang could go if we wanted to but I think we were all pretty content to just hang out here as Peter had suggested. Certainly, Peter Sullivan and Marcia Gideon would be staying. And as I cruised by my VW bus, I saw the shades were drawn and I could hear amorous noises coming from inside. Probably Zola and Frank. Zola usually didn't waste much time. Life's too short as she always said.

I scoped out a comfortable couch away from the remaining partiers, lay down and closed my eyes to think. I was thinking about the evolution revolu-

tion and all that it could mean to our group, to our lives, and more personally, to me. I was thinking about other things too, but Revolution kept drumming in my head, louder and louder. I awoke with a bit of a start, trying to figure out where I was. But Revolution was still beating in my head. Was I still dreaming? No, I realized as I discovered it was just the Beatles singing on the state-of-the-art reel to reel tape player that Peter Sullivan had installed in the house and had set to play over and over.

I guess I had done more sleeping than thinking because it was daylight. As I looked around, it appeared I was the first to awaken. Other folks were lying around both in the house and outside by the pool. And I knew there were several bedrooms upstairs in the big house, as well.

I collected myself and went in search of coffee, but mostly I just needed to move around and get my bearings. As I wandered into the kitchen, I saw I was not the first to wake up after all. Someone was standing over the stove. I spied the full coffee pot next to him and made my move.

"Hi," I said. "I don't think I met you last night, I'm Zeke."

"Wasn't here last night," the guy said casually. "My name is Neil. Just came in a little while ago. I usually help Peter clean up and cook up something after he has a big party."

Wow, I thought. Now I knew Peter Sullivan had it made. He even had people clean up after him.

"Have a seat," said Neil. "I've got some French toast and bacon all ready for you. See what you think."

I accepted the plate and thanked him. "This looks great," I said, shoving in a bite between sips of coffee. "And it is great. Wow, best I've had."

"Thanks," Neil said. "I just tried a new recipe."

"So how do you know Peter?" I asked.

"I'm actually friends with his sister," said Neil. "We met in culinary school and have been friends for almost a year. Of course, the last three

months she's been off in France, learning all kinds of cooking skills that I'm probably not. But we keep in touch and Peter's place is like a second home to me now."

"Didn't know Peter had a sister," I said, realizing that I really didn't know much about Peter Sullivan at all. Rich asshole about summed up my knowledge of him.

"Yeah, she's a year or so younger, and has a much better personality," Neil said under his breath. "Not that I have a problem with Peter. He just takes some getting used to. So, do you know him from school?"

"Yeah," I said, trying to decide whether the breakfast or the conversation was most important. Neil and I talked a little more, but as other guests came in to try some of the great breakfast, I went in search of Paula. She was just waking up and stretching and, honestly, looked a little rough.

'Wow, what a night," she said, wiping at her eyes before she found her glasses. "A good time, but I'm not used to this much partying."

I agreed, although I felt pretty good after Neil's breakfast. I directed Paula to the kitchen and promised her that Neil would fix her right up.

Peter and Marcia arrived next, looking happy as could be. Well, I thought, a success for some of us.

We sat around with coffee for a while and then started making motions to leave. Seemed as if Frank and Zola had cleared out of the bus so we were good to go.

"Thanks Peter," I said at the door. "A great party and an awesome place you have here."

"No problem man," said Peter with a huge grin. "Come by anytime you want. All of you are welcome to just come and hang out."

So that's what we did, all through the rest of our sophomore year. People came and went and a few more were added to the loosely formed group. We *all got along pretty well. And surprisingly, Frank and Zola stayed together for the rest of the year, as did Peter and Marcia.*

Good days.

CHAPTER THREE

"Hey Ziggy, are you awake?" asked Al as he stepped onto Ziggy's boat. "I've been working on the houseboat and it's really coming along. Come on over and take a look."

Ziggy was awake, just not ready for company, but he got himself together and headed down to Al's boat, a short walk from his place. Al had taken over ownership of his new home about two months ago and Ziggy hadn't been down in a while, so he was anxious to see what Al had done to the old tub.

"Amazing man!" Ziggy shouted as he stepped aboard. "Doesn't even look like the same place. How'd you manage all this?"

"Well, my son-in-law and a couple of his firefighter buddies came down for four or five days and helped me out," Al said proudly. "Didn't really cost me much and it feels so good to be over the worst of it."

There really was a change. They'd carved out a bedroom space and a little kitchen/living area inside the small place. Sure, it was tight, but what Al showed him next made up for it.

"Can you manage these stairs, Ziggy?" asked Al as he gestured toward a ladder in the middle of the living area.

"Sure, I guess so, if it's going to be worth it," Ziggy said skeptically.

"Oh, it's worth it," Al grinned and hustled up the ladder ahead of him.

When he got to the top, Ziggy had to take a breath. Not from the climb but from the view. Those guys had built a beautiful party deck topside with a 360-degree view.

"Wow Al, I guess the next party will be here for sure!" Ziggy said, heading for a deck chair. "This is awesome."

"And it's all tricked out too, compliments of my son-in-law and his buddies," said Al as he reached into a small fridge and pulled out a Sprite for him and a brew for his pal.

There were some tables and chairs and even a little bar set up. Ziggy could tell that Al was pretty proud of it all. He kept moving around from one area to another, talking the whole time.

They sat up there for at least an hour, just enjoying life and each other's company. The water was calm and from their vantage point, they could see the boating traffic and even a few fishermen out on the river. At that moment in their lives, they were content with what they had and where they were. Despite all the ups and downs, life was good.

"So, we should really have a party," said Al eagerly. "I was thinking about a sort of reunion, you know. We could try to track down some of the old gang, and we've got a few friends from around this community, you know, like Chuck and Stu and Audrey," he said, referring to the two brothers and their sister who lived just a little farther down the dock. "It could be fun; certainly interesting."

Ziggy closed his eyes to think. "Well, I don't know. You know what they say about not being able to go home again. Don't know if we even could track any of the old gang down," he mused.

"Sure we could," Al said, undaunted. "We can go to the library and use their computers and Google the shit out of those folks. We're bound to come up with some leads, right? And wouldn't it be great to see every-one…just like the old days?"

"Yeah, but now we're all in our golden days and it might be a little strange," Ziggy said, still with his eyes closed. "And even if we could track them down, who knows if they'd want to get together…a bunch of old farts?" Ziggy really had only been half listening at that point. He figured

Al would do his usual thing and move on from the subject, then get on to something new. But he didn't.

"Well, I say let's give it a try," Al persisted. "What can it hurt?"

Ziggy just sighed and said, "Yeah, what can it hurt?"

CHAPTER FOUR

"**I**t hurts!" screamed Ziggy.

"What's the matter man?" asked Al. "What hurts?"

"My head man," sighed Ziggy. "This is messing with my head."

The pair was sitting at the dining table in Ziggy's houseboat, with several shoeboxes scattered around them.

"Well, if we're going to track down folks, we have to try to find our latest data," Al said. "How long have you had all this stuff and why is it such a mess?"

"Well, it just kind of built up over the years," Ziggy said. "When I packed up to move to Portland, I just sort of threw all these scraps of paper into boxes and figured I'd sort them out when I landed someplace again. Just haven't gotten around to it I guess."

"Hell, I've never seen such a mess," said Al. "If I was still a drinking man, this for sure would drive me to drink. Let's try to figure out some order to all this."

The two worked right through lunch, with only one break for a joint (to clear their heads, maybe). Finally, they had narrowed all the scraps to three piles: dead, dead end, and possibility.

"Well the good news is that our 'dead' pile is smaller than the other two," said Al with a smile.

"That's probably only because half of the 'possibility' scraps will probably go into that pile eventually," said Ziggy.

"Stop being so damn negative about all this," Al chided. "This is a good project and I just know we're going to be able to track down some of these folks."

"Hey Al," Ziggy said. "How come we're just going through my stuff and I'm getting all the grief? Where is your contact shoebox?"

"I, my fine Zig, am an organized man," answered Al with a smile. "And, as soon as we fix ourselves a sandwich and beverage, I'll show you what I've got. It's not a bunch of scraps like yours. It's all in one place, my little black book."

After satisfying their hunger, Ziggy and Al thought about heading out to the store, or visiting a neighbor, or anything but going back to their seemingly impossible job. However, the rain outside was as daunting as their task at hand.

"Let's just give it another hour," Al said. "I've got to work tonight so I should probably take a nap so I can stay alert. One more hour, OK Ziggy?"

"OK," said Ziggy, "But only if we can look at your little black book instead of my shoeboxes of scraps."

Ziggy reached for Al's address book and Al snatched it back.

"No way pal, this is all mine. It's a valuable little book. And so organized," said Al, as he started to thumb through the pages. "Now, it's not organized in the traditional way, you know ABC, etc. It's organized in 'Al the Man's' way."

Ziggy remembered that no one called Al 'Al the Man' except Al himself. It had been that way for as long as Ziggy had known him.

"See here is the section of 'lady friends I'm still friends with;' and here's the pages with 'lady friends I've lost track of,' and this last section is 'lady friends I've married'," Al said with a smile.

"Married?" asked Ziggy. "I thought you only fell into that marriage thing once in your life. When did you have time to marry all these women? There must be at least a dozen of them!" Ziggy started to think maybe Al was 'the man.'

"No Ziggy," Al said, laughing. "I married them, as in officiating. Remember when a bunch of us sent for those Universal Life minister certificates? It was a stab at keeping out of the draft, but turns out we really were official ministers — could marry people. So, I did. About half of the marriages turned out okay, as far as I know. At least as well as mine did."

"Yeah, when you finally settled down to one woman, I thought it was working out pretty good," Ziggy said. "I liked Joan the only time I met her. And from the sounds of it you got a great kid and grandkids out of the deal. And now, a son-in-law with buddies who will come down and pitch in on projects. Not bad Al, until you messed up." Ziggy recalled a rather messy divorce and it was around then that he and Al sort of lost touch.

"Truth be told, it was all my fault, I guess," Al admitted. "Couldn't stay away from the women and the drinking. Well, I gave up the drinking but I still love me my women," he said as he looked at the section in his black book that listed lady friends he still got along with. "Now here's a blast from the past Ziggy. Remember Mona? Cute little thing, loved her for at least six months. Aside from that one pregnancy scare, we had some pretty good times together. She's still in San Francisco, so she's not too far away." Al started to scratch his head thoughtfully. "And I do believe she's a widow lady now. Her husband died a few years back, cancer got him. For sure I'm going to invite Mona."

"Didn't she tell you she never wanted to see your lying cheating face again?" asked Ziggy. "I seem to remember a big knock-down-drag-out discussion when you guys broke up."

"Oh sure, but that was a long time ago. Look how much we've forgotten over the years. I'm sure it's the same with Mona. She's definitely on the list," said Al, closing his black book and shoving it in his pocket. "Well, that's it for me today. Gotta go grab a few Z's before I head over to work. You could still work on your piles though," he said as he thumbed through the 'dead' pile they'd made. "You know a lot of these dead ones died in Vietnam; way too young to be in that pile. There were a lot of casualties back then, remember Ziggy?" he asked as he wandered onto the dock and headed back to his place.

"Yeah," agreed Ziggy to the empty doorway. He looked at his piles of scraps, and then decided to take a short nap himself. "A lot of casualties back then."

CHAPTER FIVE

War didn't cause all the casualties during our last two years in college. It was the era of "turn on, tune in, drop out," and many of our friends and acquaintances did just that in their own ways. Drugs were big on campus then and easy to get. A lot of us didn't have much money so we relied on the "kindness of friends" when we wanted to experiment. Of course, over at Peter Sullivan's house, there was always something to drop, smoke or drink and we all continued to spend a lot of time over there. Marcia had pretty much moved in with Peter and they were still going strong. While many of us guys were trying to keep up our grades, with one eye on our draft numbers, a lot of the girls just hung out and partied a lot more than they used to. That led to some casualties, my best friend Paula being one of them.

I'd noticed that Paula had been doing a lot more drinking while we were out, at Peter's or wherever. And it seemed that if she wasn't in class, she was getting high on something. "It's all good, Zeke," she'd say. Of course, if she'd had too much of whatever, it would come out, "Ish all good Zik, I mean Zikky, or is it Ziggy?" So, out of Paula's stupor came my movement from Zeke to Ziggy. Sounded a lot more hip to me and everyone seemed to jump on board with it. Of course, Paula never did remember that she was the one who started it all.

We talked about her indulgences once in a while when she was straight, but that was hardly ever. We all worried about her, but she claimed she could handle it and wasn't particularly concerned. Sadly, that proved untrue a few months later.

"Hey guys come on!" shouted Ned as he burst into the kitchen at Peter's house. A bunch of us were just deciding what kind of pizza to order for lunch. "There's a big demonstration going on at Berkeley this afternoon," he announced, referring to the University.

"There's always a big demonstration going on at Berkeley," said Frank, who was entertaining us on the guitar.

"But this is a really big one; we have to go let our voices be heard about this damn war," Ned persisted. "You guys need to get more involved!"

It had been a lazy, hazy Saturday morning for most of us. We were just involved in ordering our pizza and hanging around the pool with a couple of beers. Finals were the next week and we were all trying to put off studying for just a little bit longer.

"I'll go with you," said Paula brightly. "I need some 'stimulation' if you know what I mean. Will there be any stimulation over there, Ned?"

We all knew what Paula meant and Ned did too, but he just shrugged and said, "I guess so. If you're coming, we'd better head out now because parking will be a problem and we want to pick up our protest signs."

"Sure, let's go," said Paula as she reached into the refrigerator for a couple cans of beer. "I'll bring a little perk-me-up for the road."

And off they went, just the two of them, with all of the rest of us shaking our heads. Ned was gung-ho about the war and a bunch of other slights he felt our generation was getting, and participated in as many rallies and demonstrations as he could. But Paula had only been out for a good time lately, and we worried about her at Berkeley. But soon we were sitting by the pool, finishing up the pizza and contemplating hitting the books. Sunday for sure, we told ourselves.

Saturday night came and went and I was true to my word...I studied all Sunday morning and into the afternoon. When I decided enough was enough, I headed over to Paula's place to see if she wanted to hang out. She had a room at a boarding house just off the campus grounds. Got there, no Paula. I figured she might be at the library or something and decided to just head over to Peter's house to watch some baseball on his big color TV.

I went back to my dorm room and started gathering up my stuff. I was just about ready to head out to Peter's when the phone rang. It was Paula. "Oh Ziggy, I've really screwed up this time," she sobbed. "Can you come and get me? I don't have anyone else to call."

"Sure," I said, anxious to find out what happened. "Where are you?"

"I'm in jail," she sniffled. "Been here all night, but they said they'd let me go if someone would come pick me up and vouch for me and get me out of Berkeley."

"I'm on my way," I said, not waiting to hear any more. I was pretty sure it'd all be excuses and accusations and I'd heard plenty of those from Paula in the last several months. But she was my friend and friends help friends, so off I went.

"Oh, it was a great demonstration," said Paula as I hustled her out of the police station holding room and headed down the street to where my bus was parked. There were still a few people in the holding cell, but it looked as if most everyone had found someone to rescue them. "You should have been there, Ziggy," continued Paula. "There were lots of people, lots of good stuff going around, I was having a good time."

"So, what happened?" I asked, already guessing at the answer.

"Well, Ned and I sort of split up and I started to hang out with some other protesters. We were being peaceful like and the damn cops just corralled us and cuffed us for any little thing they could find to charge us with," Paula said as she got into the front seat of the bus. "They found a little bit of weed on me and I suppose I was a little high, so they used their power to push me in the wagon with some other protestors, took us to jail, and there we sat until this morning. Honestly Ziggy, it's so unfair. I know I screwed up but these pigs are just that, pigs."

"*Well, you're out now, so let's get you home so you can clean up and hit those books,*" *I said, figuring this was no time for a discussion of Paula's downward spiral. But then she let me know that the spiral was a little more downward than I thought.*

"*Well, that's the thing, Ziggy,*" *started Paula.* "*Like I said, I've really screwed up. I sort of haven't been going to classes and I'm on academic probation. I think they're going to kick me out.*"

"*No, you're smart,*" *I protested but had to add,* "*At least you're book smart. Just tell the bookstore you can't work your regular shift tomorrow and really hit the books tonight and tomorrow in time for your Tuesday finals.*"

"*Well, that's not really a problem,*" *said Paula sheepishly. She was looking down at her hands and had trouble getting all the words out.* "*I sort of got fired from the bookstore. Guess I didn't show up a few times and maybe I was late a few times, and maybe I didn't always arrive in the best of shape sometimes. Hell, I don't know, I told you I really screwed up, Ziggy.*"

Then she began to cry. I got her into her room and she assured me she would be all right and that I could leave. I hesitated, but I knew she needed her space and truth be told, so did I. I told her I'd give her a call the next day after my classes and we'd try to come up with a plan.

"*In the meantime,*" *I said,* "*Start cracking those books.*"

"*Sure will, Ziggy,*" *she promised.* "*As soon as I get my head together.*"

And that was the last time I saw Paula for several months.

CHAPTER SIX

"Two months, Ziggy," reminded Al. The two had been working on the reunion project for a long time and, of course, Al had been taking the lead. "We've still got so much to do and this shindig is happening in two months!"

"I know Al, but I've got to get to the grocery store today and I want to do it early enough to take advantage of all the sales," Ziggy said. "Senior discount day at Safeway only comes once a week, though God only knows who the other days are for. They've got lots of good stuff on sale, not to mention I need my beer. Of course," Ziggy added with a smile at Al. "If you came along, then we could split the cab fare home and get through it faster and get back to party planning." Walking to the big Safeway store was OK, but carrying groceries back was too much to ask, thought Ziggy.

"Damn, Ziggy," moaned Al. "Why today? You know I hate shopping and shopping with all those old people around just frustrates me. All you do is save a few cents on senior discount day. Can't we do it tomorrow?"

"Tomorrow just takes us one step closer to our deadline," said Ziggy. "If we go right now, we'll miss a lot of the crowd. And besides that, every penny counts for me. What do you say?"

Al finally agreed, so the pair headed for the Safeway a mile or so away. It was still cool in the morning, but they knew the June afternoons in Portland could get brutally hot. Ziggy picked up some great bargains and even Al got into the act. Of course, Al was ever the prankster and couldn't stop himself from putting random things into unsuspecting shoppers' carts. As the pair headed for the checkout line at the front of the store, Ziggy started counting his purchases to see if they could make it into the "15 items or less" express line.

"I think we can do it Al," said Ziggy. "If you'll take my 12 pack of beer in your cart and I'll pay you."

"Hold on, man," Al said as Ziggy headed for the short express line. "Let's just get in this long line over here. I want to take a look at the newspaper while we're waiting. No need to pay for it and as you say, every penny counts."

Ziggy sighed as he joined Al at the longer line and watched him pull a newspaper out of the rack. He picked up a *People Magazine* to thumb through, although he knew that most of the "people" would be strangers to him. He really didn't care who wore it best or who was dating whom. He flipped to the obituary page where he at least recognized some of the names.

"No way!" shouted Al. Ziggy (and everyone else in line) looked at Al to see what had caused the outburst. "Hey Zig," said Al. "Take a look at this." Al handed Ziggy a copy of the *Oregonian*, turned to the business section.

"OK buddy, but let's use our inside voice alright?" asked Ziggy quietly as he took the newspaper from Al and slipped on his reading glasses. "Wow, this article is about Neil Morrison, our old buddy the chef," said Ziggy.

"It sure is," said Al as he took the newspaper back. "Seems our Neil came back from his slump in a big way. Must have kicked his bad habit finally and now has three restaurants. Says here that he's going to open his fourth restaurant right here in good old Portland. What do you say to that Ziggy? If that is not fate dropping a pile of good fortune on us, huh?"

"Well, I'm happy for him," said Ziggy, mostly pleased that they wouldn't have to put Neil's name in the 'dead' pile. "I'm surprised we

didn't come up with that information when we were doing our research."
Al had been in charge of Googling folks on their library computer trips.

"Well Ziggy, to tell the truth, I sort of plugged in the wrong search name. I was looking up Neil Johnson instead of Neil Morrison," admitted Al. "And do you know how many Neil Johnsons there are? I kind of put his name aside and then forgot about him. But here he is, dropping right in our lap...and he's going to be in Portland in August!"

Al put the newspaper in the cart and the pair finally got through the checkout line and piled into a cab with all their purchases. Al didn't stop talking the entire trip back to the marina, but Ziggy got a little peace as they each went to their separate houses to put groceries away. Al told Ziggy to head down to his place when he was through with his chores and they could work on the Neil Johnson/Morrison plan. Ziggy reluctantly agreed.

As he put away his senior bargain purchases, he thought back to what little he knew about Neil Morrison, and decided Neil might have been another casualty of their college days.

CHAPTER SEVEN

O ur junior and senior years in college sailed by. I saw and heard of Paula occasionally, but she was still lost to me. Some of our group went into the military and a few had dropped out of school for other reasons. But for most of us, our senior year had arrived and we were more than ready to finally leave college and move on with our lives. Some, I guess, were more ready than others.

"Hey guys," Peter announced to our motley crew. "Marcia has just made me the happiest man in the world. She's agreed to become my wife."

Rounds of congratulations came then, amid some raised eyebrows. Everyone knew that Marcia and Peter had been together almost constantly since they hooked up during our sophomore year. And while most of us were just looking ahead to graduation and getting on with our lives, apparently Peter and Marcia were looking even farther ahead.

"We haven't set the exact date yet," said a beaming Marcia. "Of course, my parents want to be as big a part of it as possible."

"As do mine," said Peter, referring to Mr. and Mrs. Peter Sullivan II. "We'll finish up our studies here and then it's off to Memphis to begin the festivities. After the wedding and, of course, a honeymoon to my parents' place in the Bahamas, we'll be settling in the Big Apple. I'll go into my father's stock brokerage firm and my beautiful bride will continue with her nursing career."

It all sounded like a fairytale to me, and way beyond my comprehension. Al, of course, had to comment that although Marcia was a great catch for an asshole like Peter, marriage was too big a step for him to ever consider. "I'm never getting married," he vowed. "There's too many women I'd disappoint!"

I'm sure Peter made a mental note right then not to ask Al to make a toast at the wedding. The celebration began then in earnest and we all lost another day and night partying at the Sullivan house. And the following weekend carried another big surprise.

"Hey, wake up you buttheads!" Peter yelled at us. "I'm throwing myself a bachelor party and it starts as soon as you get your butts in gear!"

We all started to move and headed toward the kitchen for coffee and hopefully, some of Neil's cinnamon rolls. The coffee was there, the rolls were there, but no Neil.

"Where's Neil?" Frank asked. Even though Neil was a year or so younger than most of us, we had all gotten to know him pretty well over the past couple of years, and he had certainly become part of our group. We never did get to meet Neil's friend, Peter's sister, as she evidently was staying in Europe to finish her culinary studies.

"Neil's off getting things ready," Peter said. "We'll meet him on the bus."

The bus? Everyone just kind of looked at me. We couldn't all fit in my VW bus and it sure wasn't roadworthy enough to go far. I looked at Peter but he just had a shit eating asshole grin on his face.

"What's up?" Zola asked Marcia as the bride-to-be came into the kitchen.

"Well since Peter is kidnapping all the boys," said Marcia. "I thought us girls would head off for a day of beauty at the spa, compliments of my handsome fiancé."

As the girls followed Marcia, us guys just looked at Peter expectantly. He knew how to milk every minute of drama and he was playing it to the hilt.

"Here's the bus now," Peter said as we went over to the front window to see a huge tour bus parked outside. "No need to bring your coffee or rolls. We'll have plenty on board."

Hey, we were still a bit groggy from the night before and like the sheep that we were, we trailed along behind Peter onto the giant bus. There were about a dozen of us, including Neil, who greeted us at the door of the bus.

"Welcome aboard," he said with a smile. "There's a buffet already laid out and as soon as you load up on food and drink and have a seat, I'll instruct the driver to fire up the engines."

"Where we headed Peter?" asked Ryan. "Hope it's not too far, cause I get kind of car sick sometimes."

Everyone was pretty shocked about that, considering all the daring and active stuff that Ryan did. I guess we all had our weaknesses.

Turned out we were headed across the Nevada border to Reno. And that was when we started to worry about another pal's weakness.

Reno was great. We thought we had eaten and drunk our fill on the well-equipped bus, but as soon as we hit the casino and the free drinks started coming, we all stepped up to the challenge. I went up to the nickel slot machines because I didn't have much more in my wallet than what Peter gave to everyone to gamble.

"Fifty dollars apiece," said Peter. "You're on your own after that my friends, so gamble wisely."

I'd been to Reno before, so knew that $50 didn't go too far unless you played nickel slots so that's where I parked myself. I glanced over at the $1 slots and saw Neil plop himself down on a stool next to Frank and Bill. It wasn't too long before I'd lost most of my stake, and decided to just wander around a little. After cruising around the big casino and doing some interesting people watching, I stepped outside and walked around the pool for even more people watching. Then I decided to get onto the bus for a little nap. After an hour or so, I felt refreshed and figured I'd better go back and party with the groom-to-be and the rest of our gang. I found them at the roulette table, gathered around a guy that had a big pile of chips in front of him. That guy was our Neil.

"Hey Ziggy, pull up a stool and watch Neil blow all the cash he's won," said Peter. *"We figure he was up about $1,000 but now it appears he's trying to lose it all."*

"Hell, no way I'm losing it," smiled Neil. *"I guarantee I'm not losing it."*

He lost it. Not only did he lose the $1,000, but turns out he lost a whole lot more, according to Frank and Bill, who had been alongside Neil most of the day. As we sat around the casino bar to toast Peter and Marcia, we made plans to head back to the bus and motor back to reality. A great time was had by all, except perhaps Neil, who was pretty quiet most of the way back to Oakland.

"Tough luck Neil," said Peter, slapping his pal on the back. *"Better luck next time."*

"There's not going to be a next time," Neil said ruefully. *"I'm never gambling again."*

But he did - over and over again. Like I said, another casualty of those years.

CHAPTER EIGHT

"Wow, it's been years and years since we've been in touch with these people," Al said. "Hell, haven't even met some of these people," he added as he was checking his list.

"So, what have we got Al?" asked Ziggy as they sat on Al's rooftop deck and enjoyed the spectacular day. "How many folks are coming?" And, how many will really show up? he thought to himself.

"Well, here's what we have so far," Al said, adjusting his cap to keep the sun out of his eyes. "First off, we've got Neil and his wife, Gayla. They live in Arizona now, but do a lot of traveling around. I talked to Neil last week and not only are they coming, he's offered to cater the whole shebang. Isn't that great Ziggy?"

"That's pretty cool," agreed Ziggy. "Wonder how he got himself out of that nasty gambling habit. Seems to me he lost everything he had and even some of what his friends and parents had. Guess he snapped out of it somehow."

"I'll say," agreed Al. "I even asked him about it and he admitted that he had gotten himself in pretty deep. He struggled for quite a few years. Credited his upturn to his wife, who got him help and loved him right out of it."

"Wow," said Ziggy. "He had a pretty deep hole to dig himself out of it as I recall. Must have been some powerful loving."

"Yeah and he did get a little help from our old friend Peter," said Al with a grin.

"What, Peter loaned him more money?" asked Ziggy incredulously.

"Nope, something even better. Seems the last gambling Neil did was on an up and coming stock that Peter suggested. A little five and dime outfit called Walmart. It went through the roof; financed Neil's first restaurant and then he took it from there. Some guys have all the luck."

"First lucky gambler I've ever known," said Ziggy, wishing he'd invested in some of that Walmart stock way back when. "So, is that it for the RSVPs?" he asked hopefully. Ziggy had really figured that this wild hair idea of Al's would have died down by now, or that he'd not get the response he was sure he'd get.

Hell no," said Al. "We've got Emily Wilson, good old Frank's widow. She said she'd love to come and meet some of Frank's pals from the old days and share some stories. Could be another single lady for me to check into," he added. "Then there's Zola's daughter, Lana, same reason as Frank's widow, and Bill from the old days. Turns out Bill is living down in Texas and just wants to get away from the heat. There's Mona, Diana, Freddy, Curt and few others from our lists. Then there's more that said they would try to make it. And don't forget Chuck and Stu and Audrey from down the way. I'm thinking we'll have quite a crowd for this reunion you didn't think would happen," Al said with an 'I told you so' look on his face.

Ziggy closed his eyes and started to count on his fingers at the same time. After a few minutes he opened his eyes and said "Al, where are we going to put all these people? This is a fine rooftop deck and all, but some of those folks might not be able to negotiate the ladder and for sure if we get 20 or 30 people up here, this old tub will just tip over. We'd have a burial at sea!"

"Well, Ziggy my man," said Al. "I'm glad you brought that up so I could spring the next big surprise on you. We have the big party room at the Yacht Club down the way, all courtesy of one of our esteemed alumni, one Peter Sullivan III!"

"Well, what do you know," said Ziggy, his last excuse just washed down the drain. "Good old Peter bails us out again."

"And get this," Al said, a little out of breath from excitement. "He and Marcia are still together and all three of them are coming out from New York for the reunion, in addition to footing the bill for the Yacht Club and everyone's hotel rooms."

"All three of them?" asked Ziggy. Now he was confused.

"Oh yeah, they said they were bringing a surprise guest, so I figure it must be a kid of theirs that wants to tag along," said Al. "At any rate, that asshole saved our butts again, if you ask me. Seems like we continue to rely on that guy."

"So, we've got a hall, a catered meal, and actual guests coming," said Ziggy. "I guess this is really going to happen."

"Yeah," agreed Al, "I guess this is really going to happen."

They both sighed out loud and fired up a joint.

CHAPTER NINE

"Get a move on man," said Al, hopping up and down as best he could. "We've got lots to do before Friday. Since we're sort of the hosts, we've got to show everyone how well we're doing and get these places cleaned up."

"I didn't know we'd be having to entertain folks, too," Ziggy protested. "Isn't Saturday's celebration at the Yacht Club enough? Is this reunion going to take up the whole weekend?"

"Now Zig, we talked about this," Al reminded him. "Some of these folks are coming in a few days early, those that are coming from a way away and are going to get their travel money's worth. And besides that, old Peter is footing the hotel bills, so why not? We don't have to show them the sights, we've got Chuck and Stu and Audrey to do that. We just have to make our homes presentable to some folks for cocktails and chat before heading out to dinner at the Outback on Friday. Is it asking too much to get you to clean up this place a little?" he said. "Mine wasn't so tough to do, so yours should be a piece of cake." "Yours wasn't so tough because Audrey did most of it and you know it," said Ziggy.

"Leave it to you to find a girl around here that's willing to cook and clean for you."

Ziggy realized there was going to be no peace until he complied and, of course, he did want to make a good impression on his old pals. He started to shuffle a few things around while Al sat back and watched. Finally, Al started to stammer and mumbled a few words. Ziggy turned to look at him questioningly.

"Look Ziggy," Al began. "We've always been straight with each other, haven't we?" When Ziggy nodded, Al continued. "Well, I sort of forgot to mention someone else that will be coming on Saturday and you might just want to prepare yourself. But I promise it was with the best intentions and I have a good feeling about it all, really."

"Spit it out Al," said Ziggy. "You know you want to, and you need to, and damnit, you have to."

"Well Ziggy, I confess I contacted Paula and she's coming in Saturday morning," Al blurted out all at once.

"Whoa," said Ziggy, collapsing into a chair. "Did I hear you right? What did you do that for; after all she put us through, after all that she did to us, to me? What were you thinking?"

"I guess I was thinking that 40 years is long enough to stew about it, and we're at the age when we can use all the friends we can get. Sorry man, but that's the way I feel and that's why I did it," Al said somberly. "Besides that, Ziggy, she's all cleaned up and doing great. She sobered up finally and got herself some help. She was a social worker for about 20 years and then retired to Montana to run a cattle ranch. She even got married, Zig. She's settled down and it's time you made some peace with her isn't it?"

CHAPTER TEN

'*P*eace, not war!" came the shouts from the regular protesters down at the Haight. "Peace man!" they chanted as I walked by, scanning the rather scruffy crowd. The Haight had started turning from a vibrant Mecca for our generation to a sometimes-violent Mecca for the souls that never grew up.

I was headed further into Haight Ashbury... to the darkest part of the area, going where the great unwashed, the great unhinged and my once great friend had been spotted last. This was not my first trip down there, but the mission was the same. I was searching for Paula. She had left her rooming house, school, work, and pretty much everyone and everything. She'd been in the Haight for most of the last year and a half. Ned said that some of his friends had spotted her the other day, begging for money and napping in the doorway of an empty store.

I had at first filed a police report, but doing that in San Francisco in those days was a lost cause. Trouble was that there were too many lost causes for the police to handle. And as long as the lost ones stayed out of trouble and away from the tourists, they didn't really try to match any of these folks up to the missing persons reports. Many of those who were missing were indeed lost — lost to drugs, alcohol and hopelessness. I knew that my friend, my confidant, was one of those lost causes. I'd been told many times by my friends that I should just let it go. Paula would eventually straighten out...or else she wouldn't.

But I couldn't let it go. I'd found her a few times before; got her cleaned up, fed and put her in a rehab center. I couldn't afford a really good one, and Paula eventually walked away from the help they were trying to offer. I'd *even gone to a church down in the Haight, begging the minister to help show Paula the way. The minister commiserated, but told me what I really already knew, Paula had to want help or it would never work.*

Still, I spent as much time as I could down there during my senior year. It all felt so unfinished. I sped through my final tests and skipped the graduation preparations, feeling as if I'd failed somehow. My college grades were good, very good in fact, but I still felt that in four years, I had failed the biggest test ever. I'd failed my friend.

Then I spotted her. "Paula," I ventured as I bent down to talk to the tousle-headed figure in the doorway. "Paula, it's Ziggy. How are you doing honey?" I could see how she was doing, and it didn't look good. "Talk to me Paula. It's me - it's Ziggy."

Paula looked up and then held out her hand. I thought it was so I could help her up, but she shook her head. "Money, Ziggy," she slurred. "Have you got any money? I haven't eaten in a few days and I could really use a few bucks for something to eat."

She looked hopefully into my eyes, but I knew from past experience that any cash I handed over would go to booze or drugs. At least I'd learned that lesson.

"Tell you what, Paula," I said. "How about we go over to McDonald's and get us some lunch? I'm kind of hungry too. We could eat and talk a little bit. You know it's almost graduation time for me and I think I have a job lined up down in San Diego. We may not be able to talk again for a while if I decide to take it." This time it was me who looked hopefully at Paula.

"Oh, what the hell," she assented and staggered to her feet. "I could still use a couple of bucks for later though, Ziggy. You know, after we eat and all."

I ignored that request and took her gently by the arm and guided her towards the McDonald's just outside the 'war zone.' There were a few curious stares as we moved along, but most of the people down here were used to this sort of sight and they just cleared a path.

"So, what have you been living on?" I asked as Paula worked on her Big Mac. "Where are you living? How are you managing?"

"You're not my father," Paula said with a snort, referring to the man I tried to talk with months ago to no avail. "I'm a big girl and I'm getting by. Don't worry about me old Zikky. I'm doing just fine."

I had pretty much lost my appetite and slid my uneaten sandwich and fries over to Paula, who immediately started to work on them. I didn't want to anger her, drive her away, so I tried another tack.

"Everyone says Hi," I tried. "Peter and Marcia are still together; in fact, they're getting married after graduation. Zola and Frank split up, but they're still friends and Al is still pretending to be 'Al the Man' to anyone who will believe it. Freddy and a couple of other guys bit the bullet, so to speak, and went into the military. And Ned's still talking about finding his way to Canada. Neil's still around, although he dropped out of culinary school. He's still cooking for all of us and has a job at a restaurant over in Oakland. He's working on, uh, a few issues." I figured I didn't need to discuss one addict with another, so stopped right there. "Peter's throwing a big graduation party at his place in a couple of weeks— sort of a farewell before he moves on with his life and with Marcia. Everyone is going their separate ways, which is kind of sad in a way, but kind of exciting too. Do you have any plans Paula? Anything you want to talk about?" I tried.

"No plans, no sir, just hanging with my friends, just getting high and getting by. Say Ziggy, I've got to get back to my doorway or someone will move in. What about a few bucks for an old friend?"

She even stood up to give me a big hug and looked pleadingly into my eyes. But I forced myself to shake my head and say "No money Paula, but how about I come around in a few days and we go down to the Wharf for a real lunch. How would that be?"

"That would be pity, Zikky, and I don't need your pity. Thought you might be willing to give me a few bucks, but big college graduate can't spare that

for an old friend. So why don't you just take off and give me some peace. Just take yourself back to your friends and leave me in peace."

With that, Paula walked out the door. I later discovered that she had also walked out with my wallet. That was the last straw and the last time I intended to see Paula, but it turned out I was mistaken.

The graduation celebration at Peter Sullivan's house was in full swing. Those few that had not just graduated were toasting the recently capped and gowned and toasting their own upcoming graduations. Heck, we were toasting everything and everybody. It was probably one of Peter's biggest parties ever, which was fitting, since we realized it would be the last time we'd all get together and perhaps the last time we'd ever see each other again.

Of course, we all made promises to keep in touch, visit, get together every couple of years, but in our 'graduated' heart of hearts, we were pretty sure that wasn't going to happen. Christmas cards maybe until addresses got old and we got older. Hard to believe that we could get even more involved with ourselves, but that's what the future makes you do. What it all boiled down to was taking care of ourselves, and most of us felt like we were doing a pretty good job.

"Well folks," Peter started a toast. "I've loved seeing you. Some of you I've loved seeing you come and some of you I loved seeing you go. Just kidding of course. As my bride to be and I travel down our path, I'm sure we'll think of you often (if we're not too busy)."

Peter was still the king of assholes, but we loved him. It would be strange not to all get together at his place and enjoy each other's company. We'd helped each other through tough times and we'd rejoiced with each other through the good times. And we were certainly rejoicing that night.

I was off to an engineering job in San Diego. Get a little warmer weather down south and the pay was good. Al was going to hang around the Bay Area. His engineering degree led him to the marine industry and business was booming. So was his love life, so he thought he'd stay where the jobs and the women were. Neil was going to find the best cooking job he could get, considering his debts and issues. Zola was going to Hollywood, sure that she could make it big in films (or at least hook up with someone big in films). Frank had graduated a year earlier and was working in his dad's construction company in Seattle, but he made a special trip down to Oakland for the big shindig.

Bill and Ned had a year to go before graduating. Both were still worried about the draft and Ned was already making plans to move to Canada if necessary. Bill had hooked up with a Berkeley girl and wasn't quite sure where that would lead him. And Ryan had taken a teaching job in Colorado. He said that way he could be close to the mountains and skiing and perhaps coach a little bit on the side.

Most all of us had grand plans. With our degrees in hand, we were ready to face the world. We left unspoken of the friends that weren't celebrating with us, but wished them well. I knew Paula was on a lot of our minds, but no one talked about her.

"I wonder where we'll all be in 20 years?" said Al. "Hell, I wonder where we'll be in 30 or 40 years," he laughed.

We all laughed with him, knowing that we would never get that old.

CHAPTER ELEVEN

Ziggy presented himself at Al's boat and asked loudly, "Permission to come aboard?" After he ordered Al off his boat the day before, Ziggy had done some hard thinking. He knew it was time to make peace with the situation with Paula. He needed to do it for himself to be able to finally move on. He had tried to put it out of his mind as he had done with so many things in the past, but he knew he couldn't, shouldn't. It had festered into something even worse than it really was, Ziggy thought. And he needed to rethink it in order to get some closure. But it still scared the hell out of him to go back to those dark days in his and Paula's lives.

Al came out the door with a beer in his hand and a grin on his face. "Welcome aboard, pal," he said as he handed Ziggy the beer. "I was hoping you'd come around. You know I'm damn sorry to have upset you yesterday."

"It's me who is sorry," said Ziggy. "Guess it just caught me off guard, out of the blue like that. I knew this reunion thing would stir up memories, but I was sort of pushing them down and it was wrong to take it out on you. You did the right thing Al, just caught this stodgy old guy off guard." Ziggy smiled and touched his beer to Al's Sprite can, and asked "Are we OK?"

"We sure are," said Al. "Now let's get busy and prepare for this weekend."

"Sure, Al," Ziggy said. "If I'm prepared to see Paula, I guess I can prepare for anything."

"So, Bill is driving up from Texas," Al said. "That's a long haul, but he said he didn't like to fly."

"Huh?" asked Ziggy. "He was an airline pilot for over 20 years!"

"Guess that's why he doesn't like to fly," said Al with a laugh. "He must know the inside story."

"And Peter and Marcia are coming with a mystery guest?" asked Ziggy. "Wonder who that is and wonder how Peter and Marcia are doing. It's been so long since I've heard from either one of them. Are they still in Manhattan?"

"I don't think so," said Al. "Marcia said they lived in the country but I don't know exactly where. I do know it's still somewhere in New York state though. You know, Ziggy, she sounded kind of strange when she called me. It was just a day or so after I talked to Peter and he gave me the great news about the Yacht Club and the hotel rooms and all. I was kind of surprised to hear from her and she really just called to confirm what Peter had promised. Guess she just wanted to dot her 'i's' and cross her 't's'."

"That must be it," agreed Ziggy. "She was always the level headed one, organizing the wild and crazy ideas that Peter sometimes came up with."

"So, we've got plenty of booze and soft drinks, and some nifty appetizers that Audrey picked up at Costco," said Al. "You'll have to heat some of them up in your oven.

I told everyone to come down here about 4 or so and I figure we'll just shoot the breeze for a couple of hours and then let them toddle off to the Outback and then their hotel rooms. And of course, Saturday, the gang here is going to show the folks some sights before the festivities begin at the Yacht Club."

"Yeah, Saturday," said Ziggy, thinking again about Paula being there. "Say," said Ziggy, closing his eyes to think, "What are we supposed to wear to this shindig? I mean, it's the Yacht Club and all, so we might like have to get sort of dressed up."

"Well sure, man, gotta pull out our fanciest duds," said Al. "I've got my slacks and sport jacket all picked out already."

"I don't have much in the way of fancy clothes, and the stuff I've got from my working days, well I'm just not sure they would even fit me anymore. In fact, I'm positive they won't fit," Ziggy said gloomily. He thought about the one suit he had from his San Francisco days. He considered it his 'burial suit' and indeed it was buried somewhere at the very back of his tiny closet.

"Well, you better check it out or head down to the thrift store to find something to wear," warned Al. "But try what you've got first, Ziggy. You haven't put on that much weight. You've probably gotten shorter. I know I have. Another great benefit from this aging process, eh Zig?" he said with a laugh. "Hey, wanna go over to that new seafood place for dinner tonight? I've got a coupon and everything."

"I better not," said Ziggy with a sigh. "I guess I should skip a few meals before Saturday if I'm ever going to get into my clothes."

"Oh, don't worry," said Al. "Your clothes will work fine, I'm sure. After all, you haven't changed that much."

CHAPTER TWELVE

"You haven't changed at all," said Bill as he stepped aboard Ziggy's boat.

"You either," laughed Ziggy, knowing that they were both lying. As his old college chum looked around the place, Ziggy handed him a beer and checked to see how the appetizers were doing in the oven. He had to admit to himself, that while Bill had put on a few pounds and lost a little hair since college, he did look pretty good.

"Nice place you've got here," Bill said. "This looks like it would be a fun way of life."

"Yeh, it's pretty nice," agreed Ziggy. "As long as you aren't prone to being seasick. Sometimes this boat is a-rockin' and there's no fun going on inside if you know what I mean," he added.

Bill laughed and asked Ziggy what he'd been doing during all those years since college. They had sort of lost touch after Ziggy graduated. But he had heard that Bill and his girlfriend had gone through a nasty breakup and that Bill decided to go in the Army.

"Oh, I got a great job in San Diego and worked there for about 15 years," Ziggy said. "Then I moved back up to San Francisco, for old times' sake I might say. I worked for a great firm there until I decided to retire. Then I just sort of just landed here. How about you Bill? I know you went to Vietnam and then flew for the airlines for a long time. What's keeping you in Texas now?"

Bill took a long drink of his beer, scratched his balding head and said, "Well, I really couldn't tell you. I've got a small little house, all paid for, and it's just been workable, but not really anything exciting. After the stint in the military, I was pretty messed up. PTSD they call it now. We didn't seem to have a name for it back then, just plain old battle fatigue. I had a hard time getting my shit together. A lot of bad stuff went on over there, Ziggy…some really bad stuff," Bill said.

"But the important thing is you came back alive," said Ziggy. "And you got yourself straightened out."

"Yeah, I got back alive and am doing alright, thanks to some therapy and the one love of my life," said Bill. "Flying is what kept me going. I got hooked on it in the Army and then just stayed with it. Come to think of it, I got hooked on a few things in the Army, but that's all water under the bridge now, I guess."

"Well, it's great to see you," said Ziggy as he pulled the appetizers out of the oven and loaded up his box of stuff to take to Al's place where the rest of the night's group was going to meet up. "Let me put a note on the door to let any folks know we're already down the way at Al's and then we'll head down there ourselves."

Bill grabbed the box and started to walk toward Al's houseboat while Ziggy put the note on the door.

"Hey, that boat is named after me," came a shout from behind him. "I guess this is where I'm meant to be," said a female voice.

Ziggy turned to look and saw two women standing behind him. He scratched his head for a minute until he recognized the most beautiful girl on campus, Marcia Gideon Sullivan. But who was this delightful creature standing next to her? She was almost as beautiful as Marcia, although he didn't ever think that was possible.

"Well, Ziggy Martin," smiled Marcia, moving forward to hug him. "It's been too long since we even heard from you. It's wonderful to see you again."

Ziggy hugged Marcia back. It really was good to see her still so full of energy. She had aged very well. But, who was the other woman, the one who was now peering into the windows on his floating home?

"Let me introduce you to Peter's wayward sister," laughed Marcia.

"I'm the original Delilah," said the woman, and as Ziggy went to shake her hand, she brushed it away and gave him a hug instead. "I guess we can hug, since you seem to have named your boat after me. I'm overwhelmed."

She was wonderful. Ziggy took a deep breath before he could even speak. "Well, actually, although I'd like to take credit for naming her, it was already named when I bought it. But I kept the name because I liked it, and now meeting you, I'm glad I did. So where is Peter?" asked Ziggy.

Marcia looked at Delilah for a few seconds and then just said, "Oh, he's pretty tired out this afternoon. He wants to be rested for the big doings tomorrow. You know how it is Ziggy."

Ziggy nodded, not really understanding. It certainly didn't sound like the old Peter. The old Peter would want to be in on every minute of this shindig, basking in the gratefulness of the group. The old Peter would have on his shit-eating grin and loving lording it over everyone. The old Peter… Well, maybe Peter was like most of them… just plain old.

He let the matter drop and directed the women down to Al's place where the rest of the party seemed to be. Amid shouts of welcome, Ziggy headed to the bar and made himself a Tequila Sunrise, the specialty drink Al had mixed up to commemorate the old days of parties at Peter Sullivan's house.

"Hey Ziggy, how's it going?" came a voice from the group. Ziggy looked up in time to see Neil heading over toward him. "Wow! It's really good to see you," Neil said as he brushed back his relatively long and graying head of hair. "I want to introduce you to the love of my life, Gayla."

Ziggy smiled at the pretty woman standing next to Neil. Gayla looked a bit younger than Neil, but then Ziggy found as he aged that it got harder and harder to judge anyone else's age. She smiled back and said, "It's so good to finally meet you, Ziggy. I've heard a lot about you and the others. It's great to finally put faces to the names."

"Well, at least speaking for myself, the faces have changed a bit but the names are the same," said Ziggy. It's good to meet you, Gayla. Sounds like you and Neil are making a good team, both personally and professionally. Glad to hear it."

"Gayla saved my life Ziggy," Neil said earnestly. "Not only are we opening our fourth restaurant in Portland, but we have a wonderful daughter and a super smart grandson who is in his sophomore year at the University of Washington this fall. Our daughter is a physician here in Portland so between visiting her and our grandson and checking on the new restaurant, you will probably be seeing a lot of us in the future."

"That would be great, Neil," said Ziggy as Stu and Audrey wandered up to them. "I guess you've met our neighbors here," said Ziggy. "They're taking some folks on a little sightseeing jaunt tomorrow, but you've probably already checked out the area pretty well by now."

"I'm sure we missed some good stuff, but we've been checking out this city for a couple of years now," Neil said. "And besides that, we've got some setting up to do for the big party tomorrow. We're really looking forward to that. It'll seem just like old times for me," he laughed.

While Stu and Audrey continued talking with the Morrisons, Ziggy wandered away, looking for Delilah. He thought he saw her talking with Al over in the corner of the deck.

Definitely not wanting 'Al the Man' hovering over her for too long, Ziggy made a concentrated effort to get over to them. He smiled and nodded at folks as he went, but he was on a mission.

"Hello again," Ziggy said as he walked up to the pair. "Is Al boring you to death yet?" Ignoring Al's surprised look, Ziggy took Delilah's elbow gently and steered her toward the bar. "Looks like you need a refill," he said. "Let's fix you right up. Then I want to hear all about my friend Peter's little sister."

"Oh, there's not much to tell," started Delilah. "You know our parents were wealthy, so we were treated to the finest and when they asked where we wanted to go to college, we both chose as far away from New York as possible. Peter chose the University of California at San Francisco. I think that was to sort of piss off our dad, since he wanted Stanford for him if he insisted on going to the west coast. Of course, Peter didn't exactly have the grades for Stanford anyway so U of C at San Fran was a good pick. When it became my turn, I chose culinary school in San Francisco for many of the same reasons. I didn't stay put for long, though, and decided to go to France for some real cooking experience. I wasn't particularly interested in cooking, but I wanted to see Europe and I wanted to stay away from New York for as long as I could. It worked out OK. I saw Europe and I'm a hell of a cook." She took a long drink and turned to Ziggy and smiled. "And I'd say Peter did pretty well for himself too. No one suspected that his biggest accomplishment would be to find and marry Marcia. That's been a huge plus for all of us in so many ways. So, what about you, Ziggy Martin? What's your story?"

Ziggy figured this was coming and took a deep breath. He had never shared a lot about himself, but this woman was hypnotic and he didn't want to shut her out. He thought he'd try to just give a broad picture, concentrating on the parts that he thought she might be OK with. Fortunately, he was saved for a while as Marcia stepped up behind them and said quietly, "Ziggy, would it be alright if I talked to you before I have to go back to the hotel? It's kind of important."

Ziggy was torn. He hated to give up this time with Delilah, but the pleading look in Marcia's eyes made his decision for him (and at least put off his 'history briefing' with Delilah). "Sure, Marcia. I'll be right with you and we can head down to my place where it's a little quieter," he said. He turned to Delilah, "Can we continue this tomorrow?"

Delilah just smiled and nodded and said to Marcia, "You guys go on. I'm going to head over and visit a bit with my old friend Neil and then I'll say your goodbyes and catch up with you later at the hotel. Don't worry sis," she added. "I'll take care of things back there."

Ziggy and Marcia eased their way off the deck and walked down the dock to his houseboat.

"Nice place, Ziggy," said Marcia as they settled into chairs, each with a beer in their hands. "It feels homey, you know?"

"Well thanks Marcia. I know it's not much compared with what you're used to, but it suits me and I like the lifestyle," said Ziggy. He was wondering when she was going to get down to the reason for them being there. She seemed sort of anxious and so was he. Finally he said, "Are you OK Marcia? Is everything alright?" He was half afraid to hear the answer. but he could tell she needed to get it out.

Marcia took a long drink of her beer and then blurted out, "It's Peter, Ziggy. He's sick."

"Sick?" asked Ziggy. "What is it, not cancer, is it? Hell Marcia, what's wrong with Peter?"

"The doctors are calling it early onset dementia," said Marcia. "I guess now we're of an age where we would just call it plain old dementia, but Peter's illness began about 15 years ago, and it is progressive. Thankfully, he's still OK most of the time, but he lapses into 'episodes' once in a while. It's pretty much gotten to where we can't leave him alone for very long. That's why Delilah is living with us now. She was kind of at loose ends in New York and instead of finding another job, she offered to come upstate and help us out. She stays around while I'm working, but my knees are starting to act up and I may not be able to keep up the pace at the hospital much longer. As it is, I'm on three-quarter time right now."

Ziggy had to close his eyes after hearing these revelations. "So, you're still working, huh?" he tried, not knowing where to start with all the questions he had. "I thought you'd be retired and in the lap of luxury by now. I know you enjoy nursing and all but it sounds like you have plenty to handle without keeping up the whole work routine. I mean, it's not like you need the money, right?" Ziggy asked.

Silence. Then tears... Lots of tears.

"Oh Ziggy," said Marcia, wiping her eyes and trying to compose herself. "We do need the money. You see, Peter and his father had some unfortunate stuff going on at the brokerage firm. Some of it was the economy, but I'm afraid Peter himself caused some of it; my Peter I mean, not his father. Peter's dad tried to bail things out but it was too late and the firm lost it all. They were able to take care of their clients but the Sullivan empire crumbled and the whole family sort of crumbled with it. We've been scrambling to keep ourselves afloat, but it's been an uphill battle I'm afraid."

"Well, you all must have had savings and stuff," protested Ziggy. "It can't all have gone away…I mean I thought it was a lot of money."

"It was and now it's not," said Marcia flatly. "And then Peter's mom got cancer and Peter Sullivan II had a hard time dealing with it all. And Peter Sullivan III had even a harder time. His mom died 10 years ago, and now Peter's father just had a stroke and I can't even bring myself to tell my husband about his own father's health!"

Ziggy went to the fridge to get them both another beer and then pulled his chair over by Marcia and put his arm around her. "Hey girl, you guys are survivors, you'll survive this and any way I can help, just let me know."

"Well, you and Al have helped and you didn't even know it," said Marcia with a bit of a smile. "This get-together you planned perked Peter up more than I've seen in years. He's actually excited about the whole thing, which makes sense, I guess, since he dwells a lot in the past these days. But it really has made a difference. In fact, he got so excited about the whole prospect that he…well he…umm."

Ziggy waited and just rubbed Marcia's back. He figured she needed a few minutes. He certainly did. He really couldn't take it all in. Finally, he said, "Well, how excited did he get? What did he do?"

"He spent almost all the money in our savings to pay for the rental of the Yacht Club and to pay for everyone's hotel rooms," sniffed Marcia. "It was a pride thing and the excitement. He just didn't want to believe that he couldn't come back as the same rich boy Peter that you all knew back in college. We moved out of Manhattan years ago and live in a small house in upstate New York. I know I'm going to have to try to get another second mortgage to pay for his 'misguided generosity' or I may have to sell the house altogether. "My paycheck just isn't covering everything."

"Well, hell," said Ziggy. "We can at least fix that. Once folks hear about this, I know they will step up and pay for their hotel rooms and all. And Al and I can maybe figure out a way to pay the Yacht Club on payments. After all, we're sort of neighbors."

"No Ziggy, you can't do that," said Marcia. "I'm afraid Peter would really go off the deep end if he found out that everyone knew that he was poor and couldn't pay for this stuff. It's made such a difference in him lately. He's really been acting like the old Peter most of the time. I just can't ruin that for him — for us. Promise me you won't tell anyone Ziggy, not even Al."

"OK honey, I promise," said Ziggy. "But I could at least try to help out. I don't have much, but I maybe could spare a little each month. After all Peter did for us way back when. We may have called him an asshole, but he's our asshole and we love him."

"Yes we do Ziggy. Yes we do," said Marcia, trying another smile. "So, if you love him, you'll do this for him and for me. You'll keep it quiet and just help Delilah and I smooth out any rough patches that might come up tomorrow evening. Will you Ziggy?"

"You bet Marcia. I'll do whatever I can," promised Ziggy.

They called a cab for Marcia and Ziggy walked her up to the top of the gangplank to wait for it. "It's a warm evening," said Ziggy. "Should be good for tomorrow night. The stars will be out and a lot of our old gang will be together. It's going to be great."

"I hope you're right, Ziggy Martin," said Marcia, giving him a peck on the cheek before she got into the waiting taxi.

"Yep, I hope I'm right," said Ziggy to the disappearing taillights.

CHAPTER THIRTEEN

"You're right, that was at the beginning of our senior year," said a voice from the crowd around the bar at the Yacht Club. "I'd forgotten all about that trip, Al," said a woman's voice.

"Oh Mona, I'm always right," said Al with a smile. "I remember the sweet little cottage by the lake and our moonlight walks through the woods," he added with a leer.

"Well, I don't remember a lot of walking," said Mona. "But I do seem to remember… Well, hello there, Ziggy. Great get together you guys planned. We've got quite a crowd, don't we?"

Ziggy had been heading toward the bar and was glad Al had called her by name or he wouldn't have recognized her. "Hi Mona, it's been a long time," he said while giving her a hug. "You look great. I was sorry to hear about your husband. That disease is taking too many of us."

"I'll say," she said in return. "Roy was a good man. Smoked like a chimney and everyone, doctors included, told him it would catch up with him some day. Thankfully, it took him fast and he didn't suffer too much. I miss him still, even though it's been almost four years now. Al has been catching me up on what you two have been doing down here on the river. Sure is a beautiful place. Seems a lot quieter than San Francisco, and a lot cleaner. Now that Roy's gone and I've finally got my finances, such as they are, sorted out, I don't know why I stay there. Our kids and grandkids are living back east and I'm realizing that's not for me, but I should probably try to find someplace a little quieter to spend my time. Someplace cheaper too, since I pretty much just have Roy's Social Security."

"Seems like Social Security is pretty much 'it' for everyone I know," said Ziggy. "Strange how we worked all our adult lives trying to make a living, and now our senior lives feel a lot like our student days with little money and no motivation. At least in our college days, we had each other, and of course, we had a lot younger bodies that could take the abuse we sometimes piled on them." Ziggy almost closed his eyes to think about that, but decided he'd better not.

"Well, I don't intend to go quietly into the night," said Al with a laugh. "I remember Zola saying it when were young and it's even more true now: 'Life's too short.'"

"Oh yes, I heard about Zola passing on," said Mona. "She was so much fun in college. I wonder if she ever made it into the movies as she was sure she would."

Ziggy mentioned that Zola's daughter Lana was attending and pointed over to a small crowd standing around a woman sitting in a chair. The trio headed over to see what was going on.

"And this is another picture of mom and dad and me at Disneyland," said Lana. "Since dad worked for the parks side of Disney, I think I practically lived at Disneyland. Oh, and here's mom in her early starlit days, posing with some celebrities of the day. Here she is with Roger Moore at the wrap party for 'Live and Let Die.' Mom said she really wanted to get into that movie but she didn't make it. She said there were girls lined up forever trying for a chance at being a 'Bond girl' or at least trying for a chance to get into a Bond movie. But she did get to meet some of the cast."

"So, was Zola in any movies we might remember?" asked Bill.

"Well, she had bit parts in 'Jaws' and 'Airport' but her biggest claim to fame was a small part in 'Star Wars.' That was her last movie before she settled down, married dad and had me," Lana said with a smile. "Look, here she is with Carrie Fisher, a very young mom and a very young Carrie Fisher. Mom had so many wonderful stories about those days, but, of course, well, you guys knew her, she often tended to 'embellish'. Still, everyone loved her anyway. And she left us way too soon," Lana said as she started to close the scrapbook. When she leaned over to put the book on a side table, a photo fell to the floor.

"What's this one?' asked Mona as she bent to pick up the photo. "Oh, it's another Disneyland picture, but Zola looks even younger there. And that doesn't look like your father."

"It's not, it's my husband," said a voice from the crowd. Everyone looked toward an unfamiliar woman as she took the photo from Mona. "That's my Frank." She turned the photo over and read the notation Zola had made. "The first real love of my life on our trip to Disneyland." The woman looked at Lana with a smile. "Guess this is the famous Zola that Frank told me about. I think she was one of his first loves, too," she said as she handed back the photo. "I'm Emily, Frank's widow."

Rounds of introductions followed as Emily began to explain why she was there and how much Frank's old college friends had meant to him. She still lived in Seattle and had two grown children. Al made his move then, and started talking to her about the Seattle area. Ziggy started to ask Lana a question when he felt a tug at his elbow. He turned to see his best friend from college. "Paula," he stammered. "You came."

For a few long seconds they just stared at each other, and then Paula reached out and immediately they were in each other's arms, crying and laughing at the same time. As they drew apart and wiped their eyes, they realized that they had attracted quite a crowd. First Al began to clap and then the entire hall burst into applause and cheers.

"So good to see you," said Bill. "It's been too long…for all of us," he added as he looked around the room. "You look great by the way," he said to Paula, and then stepped aside as others came to greet their long lost (and they thought REALLY LOST) friend from those college days gone by.

"Well, thanks," said Paula, still wiping tears and sharing hugs with more people than she expected to ever see again. "It's good to be here and see you all." She said this to the entire crowd but her eyes settled back on Ziggy.

"Ziggy, my old friend. I think we have some catching up to do," she said, somewhat shyly. "But first, I want to introduce you to my wife, Suzanne." A tall, dark-haired woman stepped forward to shake Ziggy's hand. She turned to the crowd and said, "I feel like I know some of you already. Paula has talked so much about those college days."

"The ones I could remember," interrupted Paula. "I know I caused you all a lot of grief, but no more than I caused to myself. But I'm happily sober almost 40 years now. I want to apologize to everyone I hurt, especially to my best friend, Ziggy."

Ziggy wasn't sure what to say, but he maintained his composure and continued to look at Paula and then Suzanne. "Good to meet you Suzanne. We never knew…I mean that Paula had married and um, well, we had no idea."

Suzanne and Paula smiled at each other and then Paula said, "Well, I didn't know myself, for quite awhile, but once I got sober and got my head in the right place, I started to sort of figure a lot of things out. I went back and finished college. I actually got my Masters Degree in Psychology and Counseling and as I worked with my clients, I think I learned and grew just as much as they did. Then I met Suzanne on a vacation to Montana, and things just kept getting better from there."

"So, you live in Montana now?" asked Emily. "Frank always loved Montana. He loved the hunting and fishing and peacefulness there. The Seattle area is beautiful, but he loved the openness and calmness he felt when he was in Montana. I'm sorry, I'm Emily. Frank's widow. He talked a lot about you."

"Oh, I bet he did," Paula said with a laugh. "Hope some of it was good. But he was right. Montana captured me as well, and after a few years, Suzanne persuaded me to retire and move to her ranch. Can't say we're really retired as there's a lot of work, but it's a wonderful life and I couldn't be happier."

Al, the ever politically correct speaker, said to Suzanne, "So you're gay? I know Paula said she was married, but I didn't figure, well I just assumed. How does that fly up there in land of macho cowboys and sportsmen?"

Suzanne explained how she had worked the ranch with her parents and two brothers all her life. "My older brother was killed in the Vietnam War, so after my parents passed, my younger brother and I inherited the ranch. By that time, the 'macho' folks were used to me and accepted me. It took a little longer for them to accept my personal lifestyle and Paula and all. But, after a few missteps, and some strong words from my brother, they learned to accept our relationship. After all, everyone is afraid of something, but learning about it is the path to acceptance," she said with a smile.

"Guess she's picked up some of my social work mumbo jumbo," laughed Paula. "It's true though. I do feel accepted there and it's all working out. So Al, what does a girl have to do to get a drink around here? I'd love an ice tea."

As Al went off to gather the beverage orders, Ziggy motioned to the large dining room where Neil was trying to move people in to eat the meal he and Gayla had coordinated. "Let's move into the dining room and find some seats before Al starts putting out place cards like he threatened," Ziggy said. As the trio entered the dining room, Ziggy heard an old familiar voice.

"Well, it's about time some of you buttheads started heading in here," boomed Peter Sullivan, sitting with Marcia and Delilah at the head of the horseshoe shaped table. Their old college buddy looked pretty good, thought Ziggy. Peter stood and moved to shake hands with Ziggy. Then he looked at Paula and Suzanne. "Don't tell me. I know your names, just give me a minute," Peter said, nervously glancing back at Marcia, who rose and went to his side.

"Oh, Peter," said Paula quickly. "Let me introduce you to my wife Suzanne. We're in Montana and it's been Suzanne and Paula on the ranch for the past several years." Paula smiled at Peter and Marcia and gave them both big hugs. She took over from there and talked with Peter for several minutes, gently catching him up on things and obviously easing some of his mounting frustration. Marcia raised a questioning eyebrow at Ziggy and he shook his head. It's as if she knew just what to do, thought Ziggy, but how? So many things about this surreal situation made him just want to scratch his head, close his eyes and think.

Others started wandering in to the dining room, shaking hands with Peter and thanking him for his generosity. A lot of them had taken Paula's lead and just reminded Peter who they were. After all, Ziggy knew he needed that kind of help recognizing some of them. Finally, Marcia took Peter by the arm and they went back to their seats. She did turn and give Ziggy one more questioning look, to which he had no other response than a shrug.

"Well folks, we're all here, physically at least," joked Al, who just naturally took over as master of ceremonies. Little did he realize how ironic his humor was, thought Ziggy. "It's been great seeing both old and new faces this evening. I know we've all been catching up and reveling in the past and talking about our future. I gotta say, my pal Ziggy here didn't think we could pull it off. But we persisted and you all cooperated and here we are, just like the old days at Peter's house. And speaking of Peter, let's have him say a few words before we give him our thanks for helping make this happen."

Once again, Peter looked at Marcia before he stood up to speak. "Well folks," he started, obviously uncomfortable, which was so uncharacteristic for the old Peter they all remembered. "We've come a long way from those days at the party house so many years ago. But I remember it all just as if it was yesterday. Oh, I may not remember everything and certainly don't remember all the names, but I remember the feeling and the friendships we had back in our carefree youth. It was a very special time in all our lives, one that can never be recreated, although Ziggy and Al here have certainly made a great effort to do that tonight. As I look back on all the good times, the bad times, and the really bad times, I have to say that the good times ruled. Of course, that was largely in part to the woman next to me. Marcia was the most wonderful woman on campus at the time, and you'll forgive me for saying so, but she is still the most wonderful woman anywhere and always will be.

"I'm happy to have had my sister Delilah in my life for so many years and am pleased that she is here tonight to get to meet all of you old farts and maybe understand more of the stories I constantly bore her with about 'the good old days.' And before I shut up and we get down to this fabulous dinner, I want to thank one of my dearest friends. It's so appropriate that he and his charming wife are the ones who prepared and coordinated this meal tonight, so please give it up for Neil and his partner, Gayla." Peter smiled then, the old Peter smile, and he began to clap as he took his seat.

Everyone stood up and clapped enthusiastically as the servers started to bring the food, led by Neil and Gayla, smiling and clapping at the same time. Ziggy and Paula tried to catch up as much as they could between all the activity going on around them. There were smiles, laughs, toasts and tears all around the table. Stories were told, food was consumed, and Peter just beamed through it all.

Paula nudged Ziggy at one point and whispered, "Why didn't you tell me about Peter?"

"Marcia asked me not to tell anyone," Ziggy said quietly. "But nothing gets by you, huh?"

"Years of training and experience," smiled Paula, as she dug into her dessert.

As plates were being cleared, the group headed back to the social area and most decided to have one last toast for old times' sake.

"Here's to us," shouted Al. "And here's to growing older and even wiser."

Everyone cheered and the party slowly began to wind down. Some were leaving the next morning to go back to their regular routines. Some were planning to head out to visit sons or daughters or other family. And some lived right there in the Pacific Northwest.

Delilah moved up next to Ziggy and said, "Well, we didn't get much chance to talk did we my new 'old' friend? We're not flying out until Monday, so what's on your schedule for tomorrow?"

Tomorrow, thought Ziggy. He had only been concentrating on getting through Friday and Saturday and hadn't thought beyond that. "Yeah, tomorrow sounds good," he said. "Why don't you come down to my place around noon and I'll fix us something to eat?"

"Sounds good," smiled Delilah. "I'll sneak away from my big brother and Marcia and see you then. After this hectic couple of days, a quiet break will do us all some good."

"Hey Ziggy, that sounds to me like an interesting proposition," said Paula as she and Suzanne started saying their goodbyes. "Wish we could hang around, but that ranch doesn't run itself and we've got to head back tomorrow. I know we could talk for days and never get fully caught up, but I think it all comes down to this. We're friends again, right?"

"Sure," said Ziggy, still thinking about Delilah and what Sunday might bring. He was glad to have seen Paula, and forgive her and himself for their past missteps. "You were always my friend Paula. You just sort of fell out of my life, but you were always there in my heart," said Ziggy.

"Well then, my friend," said Paula. "After visiting with folks tonight, it seems we've all sort of moved on except you. From the little you've shared with me; you have made no real connections in your life since college…and you opened up very little then. What's up with you? What's going on with Ziggy?"

"Nothing," said Ziggy, a little defensively. "I guess I've been busy just getting by, and it's been a good life."

"Good, but not great, am I right?" prodded Paula. "From what I just heard, you might have a shot at something with that sister of Peter's. Are you going to screw it up and crawl into your shell? Or are you going to go for it? Remember what Zola always said: 'Life's too short'. Well, our lives are getting shorter and shorter, so I think you ought to do some serious thinking about it."

"Well, that's quite a speech from someone who was so screwed up the last time I saw her, she couldn't even pronounce my name," Ziggy shot back, immediately regretting it. "I'm sorry Paula, that was unfair and uncalled for. I guess you might be hitting too close to home. You always had a way of cutting right into the heart of things."

"That's alright Ziggy," Paula said. "I was screwed up and I screwed you over and no words can express how sorry I am for all that. But I've moved on, and don't you think you should move on too? Life's too short."

She gave him a big hug, said goodbye, turned and walked away with her wife. Ziggy started to go after her when he felt something in his pocket. It was his wallet from all those years ago. Paula had moved on. It really was goodbye.

CHAPTER FOURTEEN

"Goodbye all," Al said as the last of the guests left his rooftop deck. Some of the gang at the yacht club just didn't want to end it quite yet and wandered back to Al's place for a few more minutes of memories. Finally, it was just Al and Ziggy, gazing out at the lights on the water and enjoying their first joint of the evening.

"Well Al, I gotta say, you were right," Ziggy said. "It certainly was interesting. But I can't believe how old everyone has gotten."

They both laughed and continued to contemplate the previous two days.

"Well, I certainly picked up ideas for some new women in my life," said Al with a smile. "That Mona is still a foxy one, and Frank's widow, Emily, isn't bad, either. Some great prospects if I do say so myself."

"Al, I thought you and Audrey were sort of getting something together," protested Ziggy. "You may need a lot of things in your life, but I don't think more women is the answer."

"More women is always the answer," laughed Al. "Audrey and I are alright, really no more than just friends. Besides that, seems like she and Bill were spending a lot of time with their heads together, so it may be a moot point anyway."

"Yeah, Bill was really taken with this area," said Ziggy. "He talked about selling his place down south and moving up here if he could swing it. And Audrey might be just the motivation he needs."

"Seems like a lot of folks tonight were impressed with the Portland area," agreed Al. "Neil and Gayla really like it, but they don't want to give up their place in Arizona, at least during the winter. Remember winter, Ziggy? It's going to be here before you know it, and all that cold and rain is not kind to the old bones. But there are always some bright spots here and there, kind of like life. One just has to suck it up for the parts that aren't so agreeable, I guess."

"I guess," said Ziggy, closing his eyes.

"Hey, are you nodding off on me?" asked Al, "Or are you just thinking again?"

"A little of both," said Ziggy. "There's a lot to think about what went on the last two days. And tomorrow is yet another day, so maybe I should just head home to bed."

"So, what's up tomorrow, Ziggy?" Al asked. "I personally plan to sleep until noon and then sit up here and enjoy the rest of the weekend."

"Well, Delilah is coming over tomorrow and I sort of said I'd fix us something for lunch," Ziggy said quietly.

"What's that? You have a date with Delilah tomorrow?" shouted Al, forcing Ziggy to open his eyes again. "Tell me all about it Ziggy. What's going on?"

"Nothing much, Al," said Ziggy. "I think she just needed to get away from Peter and Marcia for a while, and since they don't leave until Monday, she suggested we might get together."

"Oh Ziggy, my man, there's more to it than that," leered Al. "I saw the way you looked at her and it sounds like she might be interested in you. I wasn't too sure about her since 'Al the man's' charm didn't seem to be working on her. Thought she might be down the same road as Paula and Suzanne, you know?"

"Nothing like that," said Ziggy quickly. "It's just that we started talking on Friday and got interrupted and then today Paula was pretty much the main focus for me. It just seemed like we got along the little bit we did visit, so we'll try it again tomorrow when there's not so much distraction."

"Oh Ziggy man, here's your chance," said Al. "A rich, beautiful girl, presenting herself on your doorstep. You can't fool me. This is a date and you're hooked on her. It's okay Ziggy, I know how it is."

"No, Al. I'm sure it's just a friend thing...but still." Ziggy let that comment hang there since he hadn't really had time to process it all himself.

Al threw up his hands in frustration. "I'm going to be straight with you my friend. I've seen you back out of some situations in the past and if you do that again with Delilah, well I just may have to give up on you. I'm thinking you've had some rough patches in your life and you're just skittish, that's all. But time is getting shorter for us Ziggy, for all of us. It's time to move on."

"Funny," said Ziggy as felt the wallet in his pocket. "Someone else just told me that."

CHAPTER FIFTEEN

"**P**eter never told me that," laughed Delilah. She and Ziggy were sitting on his back deck and enjoying each other's company. "I thought he'd told me all the stories there were, but I never heard that one," she added. "Makes me really wish I'd been around during those times. Who knows how our lives would have changed? Say, Ziggy, I know it's legal and all here… Do you happen to have any weed?" she asked.

"Well sure," Ziggy said. "Wasn't sure if you'd be into that."

"I'm a child of the 60s aren't I?" laughed Delilah as Ziggy went inside to roll a joint.

She followed him inside and started to clean up the dishes from their lunch. "So, let's go back outside and fire that up," she suggested. "And then you're going to tell me all about yourself."

"Oh great," said Ziggy under his breath. He knew this was coming, but he just wasn't ready to face letting out too much. "Life's too short," he told himself, kind of trying to use it as a mantra. He took a deep breath and went back outside again to join Delilah. She was on her cell phone when Ziggy went outside. She looked very unhappy and Ziggy thought he saw some tears.

"OK sis, I'll get there as soon as I can," Delilah said. She turned to Ziggy and started crying for real.

"What's wrong?" asked Ziggy, not sure whether to hug her or back off. He chose a hug and she went into his arms, still sniffling. "Is it Peter? Is it Marcia? What?"

"My father died this morning," said Delilah, as she tried to gather her thoughts and straighten up. "We knew it was coming, but it's still hard to take, you know? And Marcia doesn't know how to tell Peter since he didn't even know our dad had a stroke. It's a mess Ziggy, and I've got to go. Marcia has us flying out on the red eye tonight, and I've got to go help her get stuff packed and get us to the airport."

"Oh, D, I'm so sorry," said Ziggy, still unsure of what else to say. "Is there anything I can do to help?"

"No Ziggy, you know our organized Marcia," smiled Delilah. "She just needs some moral support right now and we have to figure out how and what and when to tell Peter.

Sorry to interrupt our date like this," she said as she called for a cab to take her back to the hotel.

A date, thought Ziggy. She had actually called it a date. Maybe Al was right. He'd have to think about that later. For now, he just got Delilah up the gangplank to wait for the cab.

"Sorry again, Ziggy," said Delilah as the cab pulled up. "It really was a great lunch and I really enjoyed our time together. Next time I'll cook for you." With that she got into the cab and waved goodbye.

Next time? Whatever did that mean? thought Ziggy. Too many things were happening at once and he decided to go back to his place and take a little nap to think about it all. But no such luck.

"Where've you been, man?" asked Al, sitting on one of Ziggy's deck chairs. "I thought I'd come down and say hi to you and Delilah before I head off to Audrey's for a home cooked dinner, but you guys were gone. Where's your date? What's up?"

"Too much and not enough," said Ziggy, thinking mostly about his and Delilah's disrupted 'date.' He sat down and lit the joint he had rolled and told Al about Peter and Delilah's dad and how they were heading back to New York in a few hours to make arrangements. "No one knows how to tell Peter cause they hadn't even told him his dad had a stroke," said Ziggy.

"Huh? Why didn't Peter know about his dad?" asked Al. "Why the big secret?"

"Well, no one is supposed to know, but I think some of our friends figured it out. I know Paula did. Peter's been suffering from dementia, actually for quite a while. It hit him early and apparently it hit him hard," Ziggy explained. "Marcia and Delilah have been keeping an eye on him, but didn't want to upset him just before this trip."

"Wow, that's pretty heavy," Al agreed. "Guess the super-rich don't have it perfect after all."

"That's another thing," said Ziggy, thinking he might as well spill all of the beans. "They aren't exactly super rich any more either. Between Peter's dementia and the economy, they lost pretty much all of their money. The story just gets worse, it seems."

"Good old Peter though," said Al philosophically. "At least he's had Marcia through all this. She is quite a woman. And so is that sister of his, even if she's not an heiress. Now, dish about your date, Ziggy," he encouraged.

"Oh, I don't know," started Ziggy. "Not really much to tell and who knows where it would have gone if we hadn't been interrupted by Marcia's phone call. Of course, if it hadn't been that, I'm guessing you would have interrupted us anyway," he smiled. "At any rate, we had no shortage of conversation and I think I did OK with lunch. Can't go wrong with French dip sandwiches, right?"

"One of my favorites," agreed Al. "And, speaking of food, I guess I'll head down to Audrey's and see what she's got cooking. Before I go though, is there anything you need Zig?"

"Anything I need?" asked Ziggy. He shook his head, said goodbye to Al, and decided to take a little nap.

CHAPTER SIXTEEN

"Anything you need Mr. Martin? The nurse was asking me questions. "No, I guess I'm fine for now," I answered, looking down at the hospital bed. I was thinking I wasn't fine at all, but what could the nurse do? It wasn't her mother - it was mine. Granted, I hadn't seen or heard from her in too many years to count, but she was my mother. Despite all that she put me - put us - through, she was my mother. "That's what you get," she used to tell me whenever I was being punished. "That's what you get!" So, as I looked down for the last time at my mother's body — That's what I got.

I knew we didn't have a normal family, whatever that was. I had no dad to play sports with, not much in the way of friends because we moved a lot. I started working as soon as I could find someone to hire me. After all, I was the 'man' of the family, and this was the only family I had. Or so I thought. As it turned out, I moved on to several more families as the years went on, since my mother decided to take a little 'vacation'. I was only 13 years old and although I'd already been taking care of things, now I was truly on my own.

No one really ever found out where she went or why, but after a few days alone in our apartment, I was running out of food and out of patience. I finally asked my teacher what I should do. The wheels started turning then. I moved from one foster home or state facility to another while they attempted to find my mother. I just attempted to get on with my life. It took me an extra year to do it, but I finished high school and managed to get into college on a full scholarship. The University of California at San Francisco sounded so grand to me, and it was. Those college years were the best, and I gave little thought to my mother or what had become of her.

"What's to become of her now?" I asked the orderlies and nurses as they prepared to move her to the morgue. "What do I do now?" I was still living in San Diego, working hard and moving up the ladder when I had gotten the phone call about mom.

The nurse explained the process of the paperwork necessary to move the body to a funeral home. I told them to choose one, since I had no idea what to do in this strange city where my mother had spent her last days on this earth. The nurse also explained that when mom was brought in to the hospital, they found a phone number in her belongings, my phone number.

"But how? Why? I had too many questions and they had too few answers. She had been found unconscious in a homeless camp and was brought to the hospital. They tried to keep her alive, but there was too much damage to her emaciated, overused body. She took her last breath just before I got there. So that's what I got. I signed the appropriate papers and went back to my motel room to think about things.

What I ended up thinking about was what it really meant to me, and I decided to just close it all out. For most people, a parent dying is an emotional time. I felt little or no emotion. My mother had been 'dead' in my mind for so many years. So it really was no big deal I told myself. Not sure I really felt that way, but that's the story I went with. I probably knew even then that this event would stay with me forever. I probably knew that I should try to deal with it. Instead, I did what I always did in unfathomable situations, I put it out of my mind and ignored it. But I guess it meant I had become an orphan.

CHAPTER SEVENTEEN

"So, I guess I'm an orphan now," sighed Delilah. This was the second time she and Ziggy had spoken on the phone since the Sullivans had rushed back to New York. "The arrangements and services are over and mom and dad are in their adjoining urns. Thank goodness there was a paid-up funeral plan and there was even some money left over for Peter and me after all the bills were paid. Not a lot, but every little bit helps," she said.

"Losing a parent is hard," said Ziggy, not really able to commiserate in spite of his recent recollections. "How is Peter holding up with all this?"

"He's actually been a real trooper through it all," said Delilah. "I'm not sure if he totally understands or remembers exactly what the situation is, but his mood has been pretty good and he's still talking about the good old days and how great it was seeing everyone in Portland. It's a subject that all three of us agree upon."

It had been almost a month since the reunion and things were beginning to return to normal, but there was just too much going on, too much for Ziggy to handle all at once.

He'd been spending a lot of time in the past several weeks napping and thinking and just puttering around his place. He and Delilah seemed to have a good connection still, but what good was it when she was on the other side of the country? Al may be good with long distance relationships (he was wooing both Emily and Mona in the weeks following the reunion), but Ziggy wasn't sure that it would work for him and Delilah.

But, their conversations were easy and they enjoyed talking with each other. Even though their backgrounds were so totally different, they shared a lot of similar experiences and friendships. They reminisced about the reunion and the old friends that were there. And they discussed being without parents now and what it meant to each of them. Although Ziggy was not ready to share everything about his mother, he did begin to let a little out. Baby steps, he told himself.

"Well, it was great seeing everyone and all," said Ziggy. "But the best part was meeting you, just wish there had been more time."

"Time seems to be an enemy these days," agreed Delilah. "You'd think that now we're in our golden years that we would have time on our hands. But I guess it's good to keep busy, keeps us sharp, and I know we'll get together again," mused Delilah. "It'll happen, Ziggy," she said. "I just have a feeling something is going to turn up for us. We all deserve some good news."

CHAPTER EIGHTEEN

"Good news!" yelled Al outside Ziggy's boat. "In fact, I would have to call it great news!"

Ziggy hadn't seen Al in almost a week. Al now was busy juggling three women and Ziggy just didn't need to be a part of that drama. Ziggy had drama of his own. He had been busy just trying to figure out his life, his evolving relationship with Delilah and whether he was going to try to pursue it. He knew this meant letting out a little more of himself than he ever had before. Another 'evolution revolution' he thought to himself. He smiled a little, thinking of Paula's pronouncement from those many years ago. He and Paula had talked once since the reunion and it felt good to be back to being friends again and having that connection.

"What's going on now, Al?" asked Ziggy as he opened his door and let Al in. It had been raining for days and everyone down on the docks had just sort of hunkered down. But it did seem like there was a little bit of sun breaking through the clouds. "Let me guess…you've added more women to your harem," Ziggy said.

"Oh Ziggy, even I have limits," said Al laughing. "No this is really great news. I just got off the phone with Neil and he dropped a bombshell. They've stayed in town for a while after the reunion and their restaurant opening and Gayla went out and bought a house! What do you say about that?" Al finished with a flourish.

"Well, that's great news alright," said Ziggy. "Where is it?"

"Oh, I didn't get many details, but they're coming over in about an hour to tell us more about it. Neil was a little mysterious and said it might be good news for a lot of people. Got me wondering what they could mean, so I told them to get over here as fast as they could and we'd meet them at my place."

Ziggy was intrigued, as well, and grabbed a couple of beers before he headed out with Al. They decided that since the rain had stopped for a while they could probably visit up on Al's deck.

"Say Al, isn't that your phone ringing?" asked Ziggy as they settled themselves in a couple of deck chairs.

"Oh, well, yeah, but I don't feel like answering it right now," said Al. "Mona keeps calling and asking when I might head down to visit her, and I just haven't decided if I want to do that or not. Or it could be Emily, wondering when we can get together. I just need a little bit of a break, you know?"

Ziggy smiled. He knew Al would sooner or later get himself messed up with his women, and he didn't even want to ask about Audrey.

They heard a knock downstairs and Al yelled for them to come on up as he figured it was Neil and Gayla. But it was Audrey. "Hi Audrey," said Al. "What's up?"

"I just got a phone call from Bill, and guess what?" Audrey said, a little breathless.

Ziggy didn't know if it was from the climb up the ladder or from her news. "Bill says he is moving to Portland! He put his house on the market and everything. Isn't that great news?" she finished with a smile.

Audrey looked at Al, Al looked at Ziggy, and Ziggy closed his eyes, wondering if Al really meant what he'd said about just being friends with Audrey.

"That's great news for sure," said Al with a smile, relieving some of the tension that had built up. "Seems like we've got news all over the place today. Pull up a chair Audrey and tell us all about it."

"Yeah," agreed Ziggy with a sigh of relief. "I know old Bill really liked it up this way, and you two could make a great couple if it comes to that."

"Oh, I don't know about that," said Audrey, blushing a little. "But it will sure make life interesting, won't it?" Ziggy nodded his head. He knew Audrey had been a teacher all her life and had never married. She moved in with her brothers after she retired and they all seemed to get along most of the time.

At that point in the conversation, they heard Gayla and Neil arrive. And in true form, the couple had brought a plate of goodies for them all to enjoy. They said hello to everyone and pulled up a couple more chairs. The weather indeed had cleared up a little and the group was quite comfortable.

After Al made sure everyone had a beverage, he couldn't help but blurt out, "So tell us all about this house you bought, Gayla. Neil made it sound sort of mysterious."

"Well, it's a surprise for sure," smiled Gayla. "Neil told you I found this house, not too far from here. I just got sick of hotel living so it's a great spot for us to stay when we're in Portland. But it turns out it's a little larger than we really need."

"It's huge," Neil interrupted. "Like a mini-apartment house, not sure what she was thinking originally, but…"

"But I was thinking. I was thinking about becoming landlords so the house would pay for itself," said Gayla as she took back the narrative. "So, we sat down and figured it out. We made some renovations, a few phone calls, and we've already got everything rented besides a good size apartment for us when we need it."

Neil and Gayla both sat back with smiles on their faces and took long hits off their beers. The rest of the group just sat there with stunned and questioning looks on their faces.

"Well that's wonderful," said Ziggy. "Glad for you guys."

"You should be glad for all of us," said Neil. "Wait until you hear who our tenants are."

Audrey spoke up and said, "Well I guess I'm pretty sure that Bill is one of them, right?"

"How did you know?" asked Ziggy and Al at the same time. Even Al was thinking about closing his eyes to think about that one.

"Neil talked to Bill a couple of weeks ago. It turns out Bill was seriously contemplating moving up here anyway, so we just nudged him a little," said Gayla.

"Counting us, that takes care of two of the four units. Now you have to guess who is taking the other two."

Ziggy and Al were beginning to feel like the old days at Peter's place when he would play those frustrating guessing games. Peter always had a surprise up his sleeve and a shit-eating grin on his face. Neil and Gayla were almost as good as Peter about all their news.

"Peter!" Ziggy blurted out. "Don't tell me the Sullivans are moving to Portland." It was a wild guess, but some pretty wild things were going on.

"You got it," said the Morrisons in unison.

CHAPTER NINETEEN

"You got it," said Ziggy as he helped Bill guide a large box through a small doorway. "Just be careful and for God's sake, don't hurt yourself. You've still got too much more unloading to do and none of us can afford to get hurt."

Bill had arrived early that morning, pulling a U-Haul trailer behind his SUV. Neil and Gayla had moved their stuff into their place the week before and were back in Arizona for a few weeks. And the Sullivans weren't due to arrive until the end of the month. Things had been busy for everyone as plans were made, conversations were had, and even a few disagreements transpired. But move-in day for Bill had arrived and Ziggy, Chuck and Stu were trying to help, although mostly they thought of themselves as supervisors. Al had been up in Seattle the past week, visiting family and Emily. Al always knows how to plan things and then get out of town, agreed the working crew.

"Wow, I didn't think I had that much stuff to bring," said Bill, wiping his brow from all the exertion. "I pared down as best I could, but I was in that place for almost 20 years and didn't realize what a pack rat I had turned out to be."

"I went through the same thing," said Ziggy. "When I left the condo in San Francisco, I had to be really brutal because I knew I was going to have even less room on the houseboat. Amazing how you hang on to some things forever and then when it finally comes down to thinking about it, you wonder why you did."

"Memories, I guess," agreed Bill. "If we didn't save some old stuff, we might just forget some of the good or bad things they represented to us. I know I had a few tears and smiles when I was going through my stuff and purging things."

Purging is a good word for it, thought Ziggy. He knew he hadn't purged a lot of things that he should have dealt with years ago, but he guessed it was too late to backtrack now. At least he hoped it was.

"Look at me!" Stu shouted. "I'm carrying a 32-inch television all by myself! Guess some of this modern-day technology is pretty good. We may have to get one of these."

"I think we're about halfway through the trailer," said Ziggy. "What do you say to stopping for a lunch break?"

Everyone agreed. Bill said that Audrey was bringing some sandwiches from the deli down the street, so they might as well wash up and relax for a while. As the guys got themselves settled in some lawn chairs, Audrey pulled up with the lunches and a 6-pack of beer.

"Thanks Audrey," smiled Bill. "Don't know what we'd do without you." The other guys just nudged each other and snickered. Seemed as if Bill and Audrey were still getting along very well.

"So, you won't be losing a sister," Ziggy said to Chuck and Stu. "You'll be gaining a brother."

Everyone laughed good-naturedly and finished up their lunches. As they reluctantly looked at the task ahead, a Volvo station wagon pulled up and out stepped Al. Then the driver got out and Al introduced them to his daughter, Jenny. She looked to be in her early 40s and was very tall, like Al (or like Al used to be before he started to lose some height). She had long blond hair and the resemblance to both Al and his ex-wife was pronounced.

"Jenny just had to come down and see what we've been doing," laughed Al, stretching his legs. "She wanted to make sure I was staying out of trouble. Emily says hi to everyone, by the way."

Ziggy knew Al had a daughter and son-in-law and two grandchildren, but he had never met any of them before now. "Hi, Jenny," he said. "Welcome to the mess."

"Well, boys," laughed Jenny. "I'm a super organizer and I can see you need some help to get this done right." In minutes she had checked out Bill's apartment and figured out what went where and just started issuing orders.

"Were you ever in the military, Jenny?" asked Bill. "Cause you sure know how to get us moving."

With Jenny's help, the unloading and much of the unpacking was done in less than an hour. Bill looked at his watch and was surprised how early it still was. "I've even got time to return the U-Haul today," he said. "Save me another day's rental. Thanks everyone."

Bill and Audrey headed off to return the U-Haul, and Jenny piled everyone else into the station wagon and they went down to Al's place.

"That's going to be a pretty sweet apartment for Bill," Al commented as everyone sat up on his deck, enjoying the last few good days before the dreaded rains came to Portland for the rest of the year. "And Peter, Marcia and Delilah will have plenty of room too," he added.

"I'm looking forward to meeting them," Jenny said. "Wish I could stay longer, but maybe my whole family can come down during Christmas break and we can really get to know everyone a little better. Besides that," she smiled. "It seems to me you folks will need my organizational skills, so I know I can be helpful."

Ziggy saw Al roll his eyes at the comment, but he apparently decided to let it go. Al was always the organizer of their group in the old days, even if his follow-through sometimes left something to be desired. Ziggy guessed that Al's daughter came by her 'control issues' honestly. And probably a little bit of organization couldn't hurt their ever-expanding group and its various needs.

"Well folks," Jenny said. "I'd better head off to the store if I'm going to prepare dinner for the crew tonight. Dad, your pantry is pretty bare, and everything could use a little rearranging. I'll take care of all that when I get back from the store."

As Jenny left, Al rolled a joint and they passed it around, discussing the changes that were inevitable with all these new/old folks appearing in their lives.

"I tell you guys, that kid of mine will mow us over if we let her," Al said. "I love her dearly, but she just has to take charge. It seems to work out with her family, but I'm not so sure I want her meddling in my life around here."

"Take it easy on her, Al," said Chuck. "Audrey was like that when she first moved in with us. The big sister know-it-all scene. But we worked it out and now I think we're really going to miss her if she decides to hook up with Bill permanently."

Stu nodded in agreement. "Well, we've come to rely on her too much anyway if you ask me. So have you Al. Can you honestly give your blessing to this Bill and Audrey thing?"

Al leaned back in his chair and said, "I've been thinking about that. You guys know I like to play the field so I wasn't really being fair to Audrey when my eyes were wandering all over the place. I think I can handle it, and I'm happy for them if it comes to that."

The group talked for a while longer and then everyone headed home to get cleaned up for dinner. Ziggy lagged behind for just a moment.

"Are you sure about this Audrey and Bill thing?" he asked Al.

"Hell no, I'm not sure," Al laughed. "Could be I'm losing the biggest love of my life. But what the hell?"

CHAPTER TWENTY

"What the hell?" exclaimed Ziggy as he saw a small motorboat pull up alongside his houseboat.

"What kind of greeting is that?" asked Delilah as she put out her hand for Ziggy to help her out of the boat and on to the dock. "Help me tie this thing up and bring me a beer."

"Aye-Aye," smiled Ziggy as he helped tie up the boat and then headed inside to obey orders. Delilah, Marcia and Peter had been in Portland for a few weeks, but Ziggy hadn't really seen much of them. Delilah had been down to see Ziggy a couple of times, but there had really not been a lot of time to catch up on things. Delilah said they were busy just settling in and trying to get Peter adjusted to his new digs and new doctors. Ziggy and Al had gone up to the house once to see Peter and thought they had a nice visit. Then two days later Peter called Ziggy and asked when they were going to come visit now that he had moved all the way across the country. Nobody knew how to deal with Peter, so they were just giving it some time.

"So, what's up with the boat?" asked Ziggy as he wiped some moisture off the deck chairs and they settled in with a couple of beers.

"Well, I figured if you live on the river, you've got to use the river," said Delilah. "Tell me the truth Ziggy, have you ever been on that river? I bet you haven't and I think it's high time you did. So, I borrowed this boat from one of your neighbors and we're going for a ride on your river."

"I guess I agree with you D," said Ziggy. "But it's the beginning of damn November. It's cold and could kick up a storm at any time. Couldn't we wait until May at least?"

"Loosen up my friend," said Delilah. "I checked the weather and it's supposed to be a calm day today, and we're going out in that boat and you and I are going to enjoy that beautiful body of water. So, get yourself ready to go because that little ship leaves at 1300 hours exactly."

"Now I know you're crazy," laughed Ziggy. "What in the hell is 1300 hours?"

"That's sailor talk," said Delilah. "And if you don't hop-to pretty quick, I'll start spitting out some more sailor talk that might not be too ladylike."

Ziggy could see there was no use arguing with her. He had decided that although he liked her strength as a person, he thought he could do without a little of that strength sometimes. Seemed Delilah still had some of daddy's little rich girl in her, and she expected, - no, demanded - to get her way. But then he thought about how much he enjoyed her company and how caring she was about everything, and decided that Delilah was fine just as she was. Maybe he was the one who should try to change his ways a bit.

"Life's too short," he repeated to himself as he grabbed a jacket and hat.

Delilah got into the boat first and then Ziggy carefully got in and immediately plopped down on a seat.

"Is this thing safe?" he asked.

"Guaranteed safe if we stay tied up to the dock," laughed Delilah. "You untie the bow line and I'll get the stern."

Ziggy did as he was told. He was glad Delilah knew what she was doing because although he'd lived on a boat for three years, he'd never actually been out on the water. They slowly maneuvered out into open water and then Delilah sped up a bit.

"You know, this is kind of nice," said Ziggy, finally starting to relax. "Good idea D."

"Of course it's nice'" Delilah said. "You just have to spread your wings a little, go with the flow, you know. Pretend you're back in your college days and live for the moment. Makes life a lot more interesting."

"You have made my life more interesting," said Ziggy.

Delilah just smiled and started pointing out some sights. "Look, there's a little restaurant out on a pier. Let's go tie up and see what they've got. You haven't eaten lunch yet, have you?"

"I was thinking about it before someone came and shanghaied me," said Ziggy. "Lunch sounds great."

The restaurant was perfect, including a nice view of water activity and a light breeze. They were having a festive meal and just finishing up when Delilah said, "Oh oh, looks like we might be getting some rain after all. Guess we'd better head back now."

Ziggy paid the bill and they hurried out and into the boat. Lines were taken care of and Delilah made a beeline for the houseboat. They got about half way there and it started to sprinkle.

"Guess we should have brought some raingear," said Delilah.

"And lifejackets," added Ziggy nervously.

"We've got those, but they won't protect us from getting a little wet," said the skipper as she motored toward their destination.

By the time they reached Ziggy's dock, they were both drenched. The rain wasn't letting up, so they quickly secured the boat and went inside. Ziggy produced some towels and offered Delilah first crack at the shower. He wasn't sure if there was enough hot water for two showers because he had never had to deal with that question.

"A shower wouldn't do me much good," said Delilah. "I've got no dry clothes to change into."

"Well, if you don't mind wearing an old man's bathrobe for a while, you can use mine and I'll toss your wet things in the dryer," offered Ziggy.

Delilah accepted and went off to take her shower. Ziggy spent the time tidying up the place and wondering where the rest of this day would go. He sat down and rolled a joint to think about it.

"Your turn," said Delilah as she stepped out of the bathroom in Ziggy's green terrycloth bathrobe. Her hair was damp and she looked refreshed and, Ziggy thought, radiant.

"Yeah, I'll head in there after this," Ziggy said, referring to the joint. They sat at the table, smoking and relaxing, and, for Ziggy, dripping a little. "The boat ride was great," said Ziggy. "And so was the lunch. It was worth getting wet for. Thanks for getting me out on the water and out of my hibernation."

"No problem," smiled Delilah. "You'll find that I usually get what I set my mind to, so that better be OK with you if we're going to keep seeing each other."

"I'd like to — keep seeing each other that is," said Ziggy. "I'm a little out of practice with relationships so you'll have to take it easy on me for a while." He didn't know if he was trembling with excitement or fear, or because of his damp clothes.

"I will, Ziggy," she assured him. "Now, however, I'm going to be a little bossy. Get those wet clothes in the dryer, you get in the shower and then we're going shopping at the thrift store."

"Shopping for what?" asked Ziggy as he put out the last of the joint.

"If we're going to keep this thing going between us, we need a love seat so we can sit next to each other instead of at a table across from each other," she laughed. She gave him a quick peck on the cheek and pushed him off toward the bathroom.

Ziggy complied, still a little stunned. He headed for the bathroom and figured even if there wasn't enough hot water, a cold shower might be in order anyway.

CHAPTER TWENTY-ONE

"I call the remote!" shouted Al as he and Ziggy walked into Peter and Marcia's apartment. "I need to make sure those refs get things right for a change."

"Too late!" yelled Bill from his spot on the couch. He, Chuck, Stu and Peter were doing a little pre-game toasting, and as Ziggy walked into the kitchen with his 6-pack of beer, he saw Audrey and Marcia toiling over the stove and at the counter.

"Smells good in here," said Ziggy as he put his beer in the fridge, holding one out before he went searching for a spot to watch the game.

"Hot stuff coming through," warned Delilah as she moved from the front door to the kitchen with two large platters.

"I'll say," smiled Ziggy as he went to help her with her food contribution.

"I agree with you, Ziggy," said Peter from his 'comfy chair'. "That's a pretty special little sister I've got and you better be treating her right." Then Peter jumped to another subject. "Thanksgiving is going to be great this year. And any minute our surprise guest will be walking in the door to make it complete."

A surprise guest, thought Ziggy. Peter seemed to be his old self so far today, even tantalizing them with guessing games like the old days. The guys all threw out guesses, but Peter had his decades-old shit-eating grin on his face and stayed silent.

The doorbell rang and Marcia stepped out of the kitchen to answer it. Everyone looked toward the doorway to see their Thanksgiving surprise. And it delivered as promised.

"Ned!" came shouts from the living room and then commenced a round of hoots, handshakes and introductions. Someone handed Ned a beer and pointed him to a chair.

"You haven't changed a bit," said Bill. "Where have you been and what have you been doing and why haven't we heard anything from you?"

Ned grabbed a handful of chips off the coffee table, settled in and just grinned at the group. He still looked quite youthful, although Ziggy noticed he was walking with a slight limp.

"I know, I know, I should have kept in better touch, but I've been busy. And it's not as if I was in Iceland or something. I've been just across the border in Vancouver. You could have tried to reach me... Peter and Marcia did. I moved to Canada right after I graduated. I was pretty sure I wasn't going to get drafted as that was winding down, but I guess I was just sort of fed up with the country. I had been treated well all my life, no problem there. But I saw so many struggling, such horrible racial issues, the terrible health care situation, and then there was the US military stance in general. I had already researched Canada and decided I'd head up there and see if the grass really was greener."

"Dinner is ready," announced Marcia. "We borrowed a table and a few chairs from Neil and Gayla, and I think we'll all fit if we get really chummy."

"If we're not chummy by now, we never will be," laughed Al, as he sat down and tucked a napkin under his chin.

Everyone else took their seats, with Peter presiding at one end of the table and Al at the other. Audrey explained that Bill had carved the turkey in the kitchen, but the rest of the feast fit on their table.

Peter rose from his chair and said, "Before we dig into this meal," I want to give thanks for everyone here. As you all know, and I finally have had to admit to myself that I've got some memory issues. But as I said at our reunion dinner in August, I value all my friends from the good old days, and the new friends I've made since moving here. Here's a toast to both old and new friends and many more good days ahead."

With that, everyone started passing food and digging in. There was never a lack for conversation and everyone seemed to be enjoying themselves.

"So, Ned," started Marcia. "You haven't told us what you've been doing in Canada."

Ned smiled and then said, "Well, you may not believe it, but I've been working with the police, the Royal Canadian Mounted Police to be specific."

Jaws dropped around the table and everyone looked at Ned to explain more.

"I know it sounds strange, but I sort of just fell into it," he began, trying to describe what he'd been doing between bites of turkey. "After spending some time getting legally established in a my new country, I knew I had to find a job. I met up with a guy who was involved with visiting schools and working with kids, tutoring and just being there if they needed to talk. I found I enjoyed that, and since I had my teaching degree, I eventually moved into teaching at a school just outside Vancouver. I ended up teaching there for almost 20 years. All was going well until I injured myself pretty severely in a motorcycle accident. I had to leave work for a while, but thanks to a wonderful healthcare system, I recovered pretty well and decided to go back to part-time visiting the schools. At one of the schools, I met a RCMP officer who was doing the lecture circuit. We talked for quite a bit and, of course, I had all kinds of questions. He suggested I stop by their offices so he could explain an idea several of the guys had been kicking around. So…I did."

"Whoa, you and the police didn't exactly mesh all that well, as I recall," interjected Al, with a turkey leg in one hand and a fork full of mashed potatoes in the other.

"Hard to believe, I know, but I did some growing up in Canada, as I'm sure we all did after college. The RCMP had this museum that was pretty cool, but it really didn't get much traffic," explained Ned. "And that traffic was mostly from tourists. The folks running the museum wanted to start a docent and speaker program to bring the history and information into the schools and other venues that might be interested in what the Mounties actually do. It intrigued me and I signed on as a volunteer while I was still going through my physical therapy for my leg and all. Eventually they offered me an actual paying position. Didn't pay a lot, but it covered my expenses and I had a great deal of freedom. So that's what I did, and what I'm still doing some 15 years later."

"What a great story," said Delilah. "Good for you Ned, even if the good you're doing is for another country."

"Well, I've been following the news in this country and with this new guy you've got as president, you might want to explore Canada, too," smiled Ned. "I've got my own take on that guy," he began, but Marcia interrupted him.

"No politics," she declared. "This is Thanksgiving dinner and politics are going to take a break, at least for one day." The Portland contingent had agreed a while back that they would not argue politics, although Ziggy thought they all had the same general opinion of what was going on in the country.

As they were finishing up dinner, Chuck asked where Neil and Gayla were. Marcia told him that they were spending Thanksgiving with their daughter and her husband and their grandson, but that they would stop by later with some dessert. Everyone pronounced that they were so full that it was a great idea to wait awhile for dessert. They thanked Marcia again for coordinating it all.

"Oh, you can thank Delilah," Marcia said. "Audrey and I were just the sous chefs. My fantastic sister-in-law, with all her great culinary talents, is totally responsible for how well everything went together."

"Hey you guys," said Al. "If we get this table cleared, I'm all for heading over to catch some more football action." People murmured their agreement as they started to clear plates.

"So, are you a big sports fan?" Chuck asked Ned.

"Not so much," Ned said. "Not even back in our college days, but I loved the snacks and drinks and camaraderie that went with the watching, so I faked it well. I do manage to catch the Super Bowls but mostly for the half-time shows. Last year with Lady GaGa, all that aerial work was nothing short of amazing. All that stuff, way up in the air. I can't believe she was working without a net!"

"We're all working without a net," said Peter quietly.

CHAPTER TWENTY-TWO

"**T**his is how I see it working," said Jenny to the group gathered in the Sullivan apartment. "We've got four cars and four drivers."

"Make that three cars and three drivers," interrupted Audrey as they all strained to see the chart Jenny had set up. Al's daughter was laying out 'the plan'. "I had to give up the car and my driver's license a couple of weeks ago," said Audrey. "I failed the eye test and truthfully didn't feel comfortable driving at night or even in the daytime for that matter."

The group nodded in sympathy as many of them had also traveled down that road.

"But I got a good price on the car and Bill has promised to ferry me around when I need it," Audrey added.

"OK then, three cars and three drivers," continued Jenny. "It's too bad that all of them are up here at the house and none on the docks, but we can deal with it. Now we know that Senior Discount Day at Safeway is Wednesdays and Albertson's Senior Day is Thursdays. So, any grocery shopping should be done on those days. Since Peter and Marcia have a newspaper subscription, they can check the specials and pass along the circulars to everyone so you can order up what you need and get it at the lowest price possible for the week. Bill has the biggest car, so I propose that he and Audrey do the grocery shopping. Of course, anyone that wants to go with them is welcome, but I suggest no more than three people on groceries or it won't be as efficient. How does that sound?"

Everyone in the group nodded except Al. He just rolled his eyes and gave Ziggy a meaningful look. Ziggy knew his buddy was itching to speak up and try to stop Jenny from any more bossing around, but was thankful that Al's argument was confined to eye rolling for the moment. Jenny, her husband and their two kids had been visiting over the Christmas holidays and she wanted to share her plan to help everyone save some time and money.

Most of them figured they had plenty of time, but not much money, so they were all willing to hear what she had to say. Except Al, of course, but he was being good so far.

"Thank God they leave tomorrow," Al whispered to Ziggy as Jenny started up again.

"Now we know that Costco has some great prices, especially on paper goods, so maybe head out there once every couple of months, OK, Bill?"

Bill spoke up and said, "I don't see why it couldn't work, but maybe we wouldn't have to go to both stores every week."

"Fair enough," said Jenny. "Remember, this is not set in stone. I know there will have to be adjustments, but at least this chart shows you all an outline of what seems most organized to me. Now, we'll move on to medical and dental appointments. Since Marcia is our super-nurse in residence, I'm proposing that she handle all the scheduling and driving to any appointments. If you all would give her a list of the medical and dental folks that you are working with, then she can handle it most efficiently. Of course, again, adjustments will have to be made, but it should alleviate a lot of problems for most of you. Is that all right with you, Marcia?"

Marcia smiled, obviously happy that she had a 'job' to do that still connected to her much-loved career. "I'd be happy to do that Jenny, and if any of you just have a medical question, I've got quite a bit of experience myself, so feel free to ask me any questions."

Everyone clapped at that one. They figured it wasn't a bad idea to have a nurse "on call" as they aged further into their lives.

"That leaves our third car and driver," said Jenny. "Delilah, how about you taking charge of our dock dwellers? Conserving gas and trips can save a lot, so since you spend quite a bit of time down there anyway, how about you and Ziggy coordinate things at the houseboats?"

"Happy to do that," said Delilah, trying to ignore the snickers and giggles from Al, Chuck, Bill and Stu. Delilah and Ziggy were considered a couple now and it was true that she spent a lot of time with him at his place.

"We're just about through for now," said Jenny, sensing her audience was getting restless. "You all know that Social Security and Medicare aren't going to cover everything, and I want to make sure you all have enough for a rainy day, especially since we know we have a lot of those this time of year. Dad, you're already working a few shifts at the shipyard, but I'm hoping you and Chuck and Stu can take charge of any maintenance and minor repairs. If you can't manage it yourselves, try to research the best way to get things done. Marcia and Peter have a really nice computer and if you all chipped in a little for Internet and WIFI, you all can save a lot of time and money by checking things out online. And your homework," she smiled. "Your homework is to brainstorm other ways of saving and making money without interrupting the quality of your much-deserved retirement. Any comments or questions?"

Ziggy put a hand on Al's arm as it started to go up, and Al decided to refrain from comments until after Jenny had gone.

"I just have one question," Bill said. "Are you SURE you were never in the military?"

After all the laughing had stopped, Peter raised his hand. "I noticed you sort of left me out. I know I have a few issues, but I can still contribute. Besides my sparkling wit and personality, I also happen to be a hell of a gardener. I know growing conditions are different out here than in New York, but I've been reading some books and magazines and I figure with a little help, and Neil and Gayla's permission, I could plant a good size garden out in back of the apartment house that would give us fresh produce and maybe enough left over to sell at the farmer's market. What do you say?"

"Excellent suggestion," said Jenny. "In fact, it sounds like a great project for everyone to participate in."

Peter said he'd check with Neil and Gayla and that he was sure they would go for it. The others agreed and said that maybe some of the extra produce might be of interest to the Morrisons for their restaurant. Peter, Marcia and Delilah had broad smiles on their faces as everyone enthusiastically voiced their appreciation of the idea.

"That's the way to think, everyone," encouraged Jenny. "Just keep coming up with ideas, follow my recommendations on this chart and I think you'll find you have a little extra to splurge on a dinner out sometimes. Oh, and speaking of dinner, how about Duane and the kids and I treat you all to dinner at the Outback tonight? We have to leave in the morning, and it'll give you all one more chance to ask me any questions or make any suggestions about the organization plan."

Everyone thanked Jenny for her hard work as she packed up to leave for the hotel. They all agreed to meet at six o'clock at the Outback.

"I've got a few suggestions for that girl," said Al as soon as he retrieved a Sprite from the kitchen. "I should have nipped this in the bud when she first started talking about it. She's going to ruin all our lives."

"Now Al," said Audrey. "Don't be so harsh on her. She gave us some good suggestions and a lot to think about. Since there are so many of us now, it makes sense to me that we pool our resources and help each other out when and where we can."

"Yeah," agreed Peter. "After all, it's another form of Social Security, right?"

CHAPTER TWENTY-THREE

"**I**t's the soup ladies," came a call from outside Ziggy's door. "You get two nurses for the price of one," they laughed as they entered the houseboat.

Delilah put a large pot of soup on the kitchen stove while Marcia moved over to check on her patient. Ziggy had been to the dentist three days before and had six teeth pulled in preparation for a partial plate of dentures. While it certainly wasn't the worst pain he'd experienced in his life, he was looking and feeling pretty miserable.

"How are you feeling today, Ziggy?" asked Marcia, feeling his forehead. "Seems your temperature has gone down."

"I feel better, I guess," said Ziggy. "The ice packs and medication really helped. But I know I look awful. I feel like Gabby Hayes!"

"Who is that?" asked Delilah, moving over to sit next to Ziggy on the loveseat.

"You guys aren't that much younger than me," protested Ziggy. "You've got to know who Gabby Hayes was. He was the nearly-toothless wonder in lots of western TV shows and films."

"Well, I'm not only too young to remember, but I never watched any westerns growing up anyway," said Delilah. "And you don't look as bad as you did yesterday. In fact, I think you look pretty cute."

Ziggy attempted a smile at that but wasn't sure how it came out. "Well, I think I'll survive, and from the smell of that soup, I certainly won't waste away," he said. "But you know what would go great with that soup? A nice cold beer."

"Oh, Ziggy," said Marcia as she started ladling some soup into a bowl to cool a little for the 'toothless-wonder'. "I'm not sure about that. When did you take your last pain pill?"

"Not since yesterday," said Ziggy. "I'm through with them, but I could still use a little liquid medication, please?"

"What do you think, Sis?" Delilah asked Marcia. "Can we let him have just one?"

"OK Ziggy, but just one," said Marcia. "In fact, we brought a six pack because we sort of knew you might be asking. And truth to tell, I could use a beer myself."

Ziggy slowly started on his soup and Delilah brought them all a beer.

"Not that I'm complaining, but I want to ask why I have the pleasure of two beautiful ladies waiting on me," said Ziggy. "Where is Peter?"

"Peter's at home, watching the playoff games with Bill," said Marcia. "All this football would be more exciting if Seattle was still in the running, but I don't mind watching football. I just needed a break for a while."

"But everything is all right though, I mean with Peter and all?" asked Ziggy. "By the way, this soup is just what the doctor, I mean nurse, ordered. It's delicious."

"You can thank your sweetie for the soup," said Marcia. "Delilah cooked up a huge batch of it, and I'm planning to take some down to Al and Stu and Chuck in a little while. And Peter is fine, but he's driving me crazy. There are seed catalogues and brochures strewn all over the house, and now he's talking about where he can start putting out the 'starts' of some of his plants next month. I know from our experiences in New York that those little cups of dirt and seeds will be all over the house and probably in Bill's and Delilah's apartments, too. It's good to see him so excited, but we may have let loose a monster. I just had to get away for a while, and besides that, I wanted to see how things were going with you and the guys down here."

Ziggy smiled as he finished up his soup and took another small sip of beer. If this was to be his only one for the day, he wanted to make it last.

"Well, I'm no gardener myself," said Ziggy. "But I've got some window space if D agrees to take care of whatever those 'starts' need."

"We'll see how it all turns out," said Delilah. "Thank God for football. I'm thinking we won't really start seeing gardening activity until after the Superbowl. But come to think of it Ziggy, you could do with a few potted flowers outside when the weather starts getting nicer. It would brighten up the place."

"Oh wow," said Marcia. "This is something new for my sister-in-law. I do believe she's starting to nest." Delilah and Ziggy both blushed a little, but laughed good-naturedly along with Marcia. "So, I think I'll leave you two alone for a while," Marcia continued as she finished up her beer. "I'm going to wander down the dock to Al's and then Stu and Chuck's to distribute this wonderful soup. Don't worry Delilah. I'll give you all the credit."

After Marcia left, Delilah cleared away the soup bowl and sat down next to Ziggy. "You really do look so much better," she said, giving him a smile and a gentle peck on his bruised cheek. "How's the beer going down?"

"Just fine," said Ziggy, reluctantly finishing his beer. "In fact, I'm pretty sure I could have another."

"No way, partner," said Delilah. "We've got to follow orders. There's always tomorrow. We've got lots of tomorrows ahead of us."

CHAPTER TWENTY-FOUR

"Let's unload your groceries first," said Delilah, as they got out of her car with the weeks' worth of purchases for the dock dwellers. "Then we can just work our way down the line, ending at Chuck and Stu's place. I want to see their cat. She's never been around when I've been there before."

"Sounds like a plan," said Ziggy, loading up the dock cart with the stuff they'd picked up from Bill's place. "This grocery shopping organization seems to be working out okay, but I'm not crazy about this part. Maybe we can take a break for a few minutes when we finish at my place? Maybe just a quick beer?"

"Oh Ziggy, let's just get it done," said Delilah. "We can take a couple of beers with us to celebrate when we finish up at Chuck and Stu's."

Ziggy sighed and nodded. He hefted a bag of cat food into the dock cart. He couldn't figure out why Chuck and Stu had adopted a cat. Maybe they were feeling lonely since Audrey had been spending most of her days (and nights) at Bill's place. An animal is just more trouble and expense. But Ziggy had never been a real pet person. He figured he had enough trouble with human relationships.

"I don't remember ordering some of this stuff," Ziggy said as they started putting away his groceries.

"You didn't, I did," said Delilah. "I'm going to cook you a gourmet dinner tonight and I need some of this stuff to do it."

"Well, I'm fine with that," smiled Ziggy. "Now that I've got my new teeth and everything is working again, I would love nothing more than a delicious romantic dinner with my delicious D." Despite all his past, Ziggy felt he was falling in love. It scared him at times, but mostly he liked it. "Life's too short," he reminded himself.

They finished up at Ziggy's, grabbed a couple of beers and pulled the cart down the dock toward Al's place. As they called out to Al, Delilah and Ziggy heard some loud music next door and wondered what all that was about.

"Come on in," said Al. "I've been catching up on my paperwork. Not easy to concentrate with all that noise going on next door. New folks moved in and they apparently are musicians, or think they are. They may not be good musicians, but they sure do like to play their music."

"By paperwork, he means he's doing crossword puzzles," whispered Ziggy to Delilah.

The couple handed over Al's groceries and he paid them what he owed while the music next door went on and on.

"Maybe you should talk to those guys next door and ask them to hold it down a little," Delilah suggested. "They just may not be aware how much sound carries out here on the water."

"Maybe I will later," said Al. "With the airplanes and freeway traffic noise, I'm sure I'll get used to their music, as well. Maybe it'll grow on me, who knows? But I definitely plan on talking to them."

"That means he's going to go over there and find out their whole life story and then probably tell them their music is great," Ziggy whispered again.

They said their goodbyes and moved on to the last of their deliveries for the day.

The music followed them, even though they were a couple of docks away. "That might drive me mad," said Ziggy.

"I kind of like it," Delilah said. "It feels like the community is singing to us. It reminds me of a quote from your favorite guy, Joseph Campbell: 'Love is friendship set to music.'"

Ziggy did remember that quote and decided he'd have to think about it...later. We'll see how it goes, he thought, as they stopped at Chuck, Stu and Audrey's houseboat. They knew Audrey wasn't there because they had just seen her up at Bill's place. But Stu and Chuck were nowhere to be found.

"The door is unlocked so they can't be far," said Ziggy. "Let's just unload the cold stuff in the fridge and we can sit out on their deck with our beers and wait for them to show up."

As they were putting things into the refrigerator, Delilah spied the cat, a little Calico. "I think her name is Spot," said Ziggy. "She's pretty shy," he added, as Delilah tried to approach her. The cat scurried off, so they took their beers and headed outside to the deck.

"This is kind of nice, isn't it Ziggy?" asked Delilah. "We're working together and for the good of the group. I feel useful."

"Oh D, you're very useful," protested Ziggy. "For all you do for Peter and Marcia and, well, for all of us. You have a kind heart and a strong sense of family. It's one of the things I love about you." Whoops, he thought. He had just used the "L" word. Another thing he'd have to think about...later.

They clinked their beer cans together and sat quietly, listening to the music. It didn't sound as loud, or as bad, from farther away. They had just about given up on waiting when Chuck and Stu came bursting onto the houseboat.

"Wow! That was fun!" said Chuck, heading for the refrigerator to get everyone a beer. "Those folks aren't the greatest musicians, but I was enjoying myself. How about you, Stu?" he asked his brother.

"It was good," agreed Stu. "You were enjoying it because you were able to join in. Borrowing one of their guitars is fine, but you better dig out your own guitar if you're going to get back into practice. And maybe I'll dust off my bongos."

"What's up. you guys?" asked Delilah. "Where have you been?"

"We were down at our new neighbors, actually Al's new neighbors," said Stu. "Nice couple, names of Moon and Turtle. They moved up here from San Diego. They were in a band down there with a few folks their age and they're hoping to start the same kind of band around here."

"Moon and Turtle - what kind of names are those?" asked Ziggy. "Sounds like real throwbacks to the 60s. They must be as old as us."

"Pretty close," said Chuck. "Moon is the girl and Turtle is her boyfriend. Seems like a fun couple and they invited any or all of us over any time to jam or just groove along. That's their words, not mine."

"Well, there's never a dull moment down here," said Delilah with a laugh. "Right now, I'm headed back to do some dinner prep. I'll see you back there, Ziggy." Ziggy raised his beer and told her he'd be down as soon as he finished his drink.

"She is a gem, Zig," said Stu as he paid Ziggy for their weekly food delivery. "You waited long enough, but you've got a prize there."

"Don't I know it," said Ziggy. "It still amazes me all the time, that a great woman like Delilah is interested in old Zeke. Just like she said, there's never a dull moment."

CHAPTER TWENTY-FIVE

"Wonder what this 'all-hands meeting' is about," mused Ziggy as he sat at the kitchen table with Al. "Delilah said she was picking us all up at 3:00 today, but she wouldn't say anything more about the why of it all."

"A mystery, my friend. Who doesn't like a good mystery?" said Al. "I was up there the other day visiting with Peter, and he never said anything about it. Of course, he wasn't talking about much except gardening and seeds and stuff. When he gets going on an idea, it's hard to steer him in any other direction."

"Sounds like someone else I know," said Ziggy, as he thought back to Al's big idea about a reunion. However, in retrospect, Ziggy was certainly happy that Al persisted on that one. His circle of friends had grown by leaps and bounds, and, of course, there was Delilah.

"I guess we'll find out when we get there," said Al. "In the meantime, we've got time for a game of cribbage. I might even let you win."

They played cards for an hour or so until Stu and Chuck showed up. The men shared a joint before heading up to the parking lot to wait for Delilah.

"Glad to see you guys," Delilah said as she handed Ziggy a bakery box to hold on his lap. "If you'll hold this, then I think we'll all fit in just fine," she said as everyone buckled up for the ride to the house.

Al had lots of questions, but Delilah remained mysterious. "You'll find out soon enough. Don't worry, there's no problem. It's going to be a happy meeting, with snacks and beverages and all that you so enjoy."

Al decided that he had to be patient, but as soon as they stepped into the Sullivan apartment, he was surprised to see everyone already there, including Neil and Gayla. Once they were all settled in with refreshments, Al had to speak up.

"It's great to see everyone, but I gotta know what the hell is going on," he all but shouted.

"You need to guess," said Peter slyly.

"Not this time, Peter," said Neil. "None of your guessing games today."

"Well, began Audrey. "Bill and I are getting married!"

Silence. Then cheers and applause. Ziggy looked at Al, who was unusually quiet.

"Congratulations!" said Gayla, followed by similar comments from those who had been caught off guard by the news.

"Our Zola always said 'Life's too short," smiled Bill. "So, this lifelong bachelor is going to take the plunge!"

"And our spinster sister will become an honest woman!" chimed in Chuck and Stu.

Ziggy voiced his congratulations, but kept an eye on Al, who still hadn't reacted.

Finally, Al spoke up. "What's the point man? Why not just shack up together like you pretty much have been?"

"We wanted to make it official. And we checked into it to make sure neither of our pensions would be affected, so why not?" answered Bill.

Marcia and Delilah started passing around champagne to everyone, and they all toasted the newly engaged couple.

"Here's to Audrey and Bill," Peter started. "Life may be too short, but it looks like it's never too late."

As everyone got a piece of cake, Ziggy moved over by where Al was sitting. "Are you alright Al?" he whispered.

"Oh yeah, sure. Just caught me off guard. As I said before, you know how I like playing the field and swore I'd never get married again. So, if that's what Audrey wants, I'm happy for her. In fact, how about I perform the ceremony?" he asked Bill and Audrey. He knew he had already given her away.

"Are you sure?" asked Bill and Audrey in unison. "That would be great and would mean a lot to us," added Audrey.

"It's done," said Al. "Just tell me when and where so I can start polishing up on my skills. It's been quite awhile since I performed any nuptials."

"We don't want to make a big deal out of it," said Audrey. "We just want to make sure our closest friends, - our family, will be there to witness it."

"And of course, to party with us to seal the deal," laughed Bill.

"How about a quiet ceremony and then Gayla and I will host you all at our restaurant to continue the festivities?" asked Neil.

Everyone agreed that was a wonderful plan and more discussion ensued about the date. They decided that since it was winter and cold and rainy, maybe they should just have the ceremony at the Sullivan apartment. Sure, it would be crowded, but they had done gatherings there before and there really wouldn't be too many more people than that.

"So, we'll get the marriage license this week and then have a couple weeks to prepare and get Audrey 'officially' moved in here with me," said Bill. "Neil, when is a good time for us all to descend on your restaurant?"

"We are usually closed on Mondays, so let's say three weeks from Monday," Neil said.

"That'll give us plenty of time to plan a bachelor party," smiled Al. "And it better be a good one for this courageous guy."

Everyone toasted Bill and Audrey again and started heading for their respective homes. Delilah drove Stu, Chuck, Al and Ziggy back down to the docks and then said goodbye as she headed back to her apartment. The guys all sat around Chuck and Stu's place to smoke a joint and talk about the Bill and Audrey news.

"Well boys," started Al. "You'll be on your own again. Although Audrey has been spending so much time up at Bill's that you've pretty much been on your own for a few months now. Of course, you've got Spot the cat."

"Audrey and Bill talked with us about their plans last week," said Stu. "And although she won't be living here, we'll still see each other all the time, and we couldn't be happier for her. She spent her whole adult life teaching, but not saving much. She did all that summer traveling that many teachers do, so it's a good thing she's got her pension and Social Security."

"And I think Bill is doing alright with his Social Security and pension, too," said Chuck. "Hell, she won't be helping out here with rent and food, so we're going to have to really start pinching pennies again."

"Imagine after all these years that neither one of them ever got married," said Al thoughtfully.

"Maybe they were just waiting to meet each other," suggested Ziggy.

"A good thing I didn't get in the way," said Al with a sigh.

CHAPTER TWENTY-SIX

"**G**et out of the way, Al," said Delilah. "She's my roommate for a week and I want to see her first. You'll get your chance at her, I'm sure," she added with a grin.

Al and Delilah were at the airport to pick up Mona, coming in from San Francisco. She had been invited to the wedding and, not to be outdone by the men, the women in the group were planning a little bachelorette party for Audrey. Mona was eager to be involved and Al was pretty happy he'd have a date for the wedding festivities. He'd hardly been pining for Mona or Audrey, however, as he had been up to see Emily once already since Bill and Audrey announced their plans. Emily was invited to the wedding too, but she had a grandson's birthday party to attend.

"There she is," said Delilah. "Mona, over here!"

Mona rushed up to them, put down her bags and gave them both big hugs. Al picked up the bags and they followed Delilah to the parking lot.

"The flight was great," said Mona as they settled themselves in the car. "I even managed to nap a little so I might be able to stay up as late as 10 tonight," she laughed. "So, how is everyone up here? Seems your group has grown a little since I saw everyone at the reunion. How fortunate that you all get to be in the same area and can get together more often than once every 20 or 30 years."

"And we've even added a little more to our gang," said Al. "My next-door neighbors, Moon and Turtle, said they might stop by later. They're musicians and they're not too bad."

Music greeted the trio before they even got to Al's houseboat. Al thought they sounded better every day, and now that Chuck and Stu had joined in, they really had started to sound like a band.

"Hi Mona!" came shouts from Al's rooftop deck as they approached and climbed the ladder. "Welcome back to Portland."

There had been a break in the weather, so the group decided to gather at Al's party space and enjoy the river. Even Peter made it down to welcome his college friend. They were all chatting up a storm when Al and Delilah wandered over to Moon and Turtle's boat to find Chuck and Stu.

"How is San Francisco?" asked Bill. "Probably a little better weather than we've been getting here."

"Not by much," said Mona. "You've got better weather here this afternoon than San Fran had when I left this morning. The air seems cleaner for sure, especially down here on the water. And it's so peaceful and quiet."

"It was even more peaceful and quiet before Moon and Turtle moved here," said Ziggy. "Thankfully they are almost as old as we are and they tend to pack it in early in the evening. All in all, they're a fun couple, and it kind of reminds me of the old days at Peter's with folks playing music and all."

"Good old Frank was the best musician we had," said Peter. "I know Neil liked to fool around with the drums and seems to me that Ned had a pretty good singing voice. And Ryan, well Ryan was pretty good at anything he tried, and I remember him playing the dulcimer once in a while. I sure wish Ryan and Frank were still here," he added wistfully.

They all continued visiting until Mona wondered aloud how long Delilah and Al were going to be. "They've been gone a while. Hope I haven't scared Al off already," she said with a smile.

The music next door continued, but Ziggy thought he heard a vocalist now. "I didn't know Moon could sing that well," he said. "Oh, here comes Al now."

"That was great fun," said Al. "Sorry we deserted you guys. We just sort of got into it all. The others are right behind me."

The rest of the contingent started wandering up to the top deck. After introductions were made and everyone had a beverage, they settled in to visit. Ziggy looked over at Delilah and asked, "What has got you smiling from ear to ear?" "I think I just joined the band," exclaimed Delilah.

CHAPTER TWENTY-SEVEN

"Wow, what a hectic week it's been," said Delilah as she stretched out in bed next to Ziggy. Al was spending the night with Mona at Delilah's apartment, so she was staying with Ziggy. "Our girls' night out was a hoot. I learned a lot about our circle and even more about Marcia than I ever knew. Nothing earth shattering, but interesting. And just a fun time."

"Our bachelor party was fun too," said Ziggy. "Although I think we partied a little harder than we should have and yesterday was pretty rough. But today was really nice. The wedding and the great dinner at Neil and Gayla's restaurant, and of course musical entertainment with my D as the lead singer. You were terrific."

"It's coming along," said Delilah. "It's interesting and it really was fun to perform in a real audience-type setting. We've been practicing down at the senior center sometimes, and they all seem to enjoy us, so I guess we'll keep it going while we can. We might even aim for an audience whose average age is less than 60," she laughed.

"I hate to keep calling it 'the band'," said Ziggy. "When are you going to come up with a name?"

"Al's working on it," said Delilah. "He's sort of named himself our manager, claims to have the inside scoop on places we might be able to play. We're going to meet next week and try to come up with a name."

"Well today was really a lot of fun," said Ziggy. "It was great to see everyone enjoying themselves, especially Peter. He was acting like the proud patriarch of our whole family."

"And Bill and Audrey looked so happy, really in love," said Delilah. "Ziggy, why do you think you never got married?"

Ziggy tried to think quickly. Could he pretend that he'd fallen asleep? Probably not – it was hard to fool this woman. He tried another way. He didn't exactly lie, just 'vagued' around the truth. "I never found just the right person, I guess," he started. "Or I was just too busy with my career and other stuff. Hell, I'm not sure." Then he tried a much-used strategy in his life; he turned the conversation away from him. "Why didn't you ever get married? I'm sure you had lots of offers."

"That's quite a story," laughed Delilah. "I'm getting a little sleepy, but I'll try to put it in a nutshell. My parents wanted both my brother and me to get married and have lots of grandkids. Of course, my dad wanted a little Peter Sullivan IV so Peter was under more pressure than I was. I never wanted children, so why bother getting married? I had a wonderful time in Europe. It was the time of free love and after all, I was in France, where love abounds. I won't lie Ziggy. I did have relationships, some lasting longer than others, but none really lasting. And that was OK with me. Everything was going along fine until Peter and Marcia found out that they couldn't have children. And get this Ziggy, I found out at the bachelorette party that Marcia never really wanted children. She was going to try for the family's sake, so they went through all kinds of tests only to find out it that it wasn't going to happen.

"So, then the pressure moved to me. No one wanted to make our parents unhappy, but I just couldn't seem to settle down, and I didn't want to. I never pictured me having children - Zero Population Growth, remember? I just wanted to be free and have a good time. But the pressure kept mounting from the parents. Little nudges like, 'Isn't it about time you settled down and started a family, Delilah?' stuff. So, I did the only thing I could think of to do. I sorta let them think I was gay! Another disappointment, but the folks respected my 'choice' so I was home free, right? I was home free until my big brother got pissed at me for something or other and 'de-outed' me to our parents."

"Wow!" said Ziggy. "How did things go after that?"

"Pretty rough for a while, but they got over it, then mom got sick and then Peter started acting too strange, so everyone gave it a rest," Delilah said with a yawn. "And that's how it was left. I enjoyed my chosen path and life went on, sans wedding ring."

"Thanks for being so honest about it all," said Ziggy, as he closed his eyes and thought long and hard about how honest he should be. He wrestled with it for about ten minutes and then finally he said quietly, "Well I came pretty close to getting married once." There. He'd said it. He waited anxiously for her to ask for an explanation.

Silence.

Oh hell, thought Ziggy. Now he'd really done it.

Silence. Then snoring.

Ziggy leaned over and saw that Delilah was dead-to-the-world. They'd been together long enough that he knew she could just conk out like that and would sleep and sleep.

"Dodged another bullet," he said quietly to himself, and then he rolled over and went to sleep as well.

CHAPTER TWENTY-EIGHT

"**A**re you going to sleep all day?" asked Carrie. She nudged me gently and then a little more roughly. "We've got lots to do today and the wedding is only a little more than a month away!"

I opened my eyes and smiled at my bride-to-be. We had been together for almost two years and had our life mapped out (or at least Carrie did). I'd been working in San Diego for about 14 years when Carrie began working there. I'd had a few relationships, but nothing that lasted too long. Then Carrie and I started dating and one thing led to another and here we were - planning a wedding. I was ready to vow my love and spend the rest of my life with her, but there was one itty-bitty problem. She wanted a family and I definitely did not think that was a good idea for me. Aside from all my questions about my family's gene pool, I was almost 41 and not ready to commit to raising kids into my late 50s. But Carrie was ten years younger than me, and hell-bent on at least a couple of kids. I knew her biological clock was ticking, but I told myself I was in love and really tried to convince myself that once we were married, well, she would forget about a family. Fooling myself again, I know, but, I was getting pretty good at that by then.

"What's on the schedule for today?" I asked. "Hope there will be time to watch a little football. It's the playoffs, you know."

"We've got to decide on the cake and make sure our flower order is set," Carrie said, pulling out her daily planner and looking at her list. Typical engineer, she was organized to a fault. "But I have the final fitting for my dress this afternoon, so you could probably sneak away to Duffy's for a beer *and some football. But Zeke, no more than a couple beers, OK? We're having dinner with mommy and daddy tonight,"* she reminded me.

Duffy's was our hangout then. It was a great little neighborhood bar, and we'd met some fun people there. It would be a good place to have a little time to myself and watch some football, and to think about this whirlwind I seemed to be living in. I thought ahead to dinner with 'mommy and daddy' and sighed to myself, but just nodded to Carrie. "No waves, Zeke." was my motto. I figured once we were married, we wouldn't be around Carrie's parents as much. Not that there was anything wrong with them. They were nice people and who was I to judge what parents should be anyway? But Carrie was their only child and they were also ready to be grandparents. I felt pretty outnumbered by the three of them.

The wedding plans and countdown continued and I became more and more uncomfortable about the whole thing. I definitely knew I had 'cold feet', but I started to feel pretty cold about the whole idea. I don't know what happened, but one day about two weeks before the wedding, it just hit me. And it hit me hard. "What am I doing?" I asked myself out loud. "And why?"

And so, coward and cad that I am, I left our apartment for the last time while she was on a job out of town. I left the long labored-over note that I had written. I left my job, and I left San Diego. I called the whole thing off and moved back to San Francisco alone. I deserved to be alone, I told myself. She was better off, I told myself. And then, just like so many other things in my life, I put it all behind me and started again. I remembered a quote of Joseph Campbell from my college days: "We must be willing to let go of the life we've planned so as to have the life that is waiting for us." I was hoping that was true.

CHAPTER TWENTY-NINE

"So, the broccoli will go here, and then I'll put the green beans back along here, and the lettuce and spinach will go in the front," Peter explained as he pointed to the chart he'd laid out on Ziggy's kitchen table.

Ziggy had just been hanging out at home when Peter showed up with his giant chart and a whole lot to say. Ziggy was trying to act interested in all of Peter's plans, but kept wondering how long he was going to have to listen to him go on and on and on about his giant garden project. Might as well be listening to Al's daughter, he thought. He tried asking a few questions to keep Peter happy, but then he suddenly realized that Peter must have come down to the docks alone.

"Say, Peter," started Ziggy. "How did you get down here, anyway? Did Delilah or Marcia or Bill drop you off?"

"Huh?" Peter glanced up from his chart, with a surprised look on his face. "I guess I took a taxi or something. I know I had to explain how to get here."

Ziggy began to get a little worried. "But someone knows where you are, right?" he asked. "I mean, does anyone know where you are?"

Peter just smiled. "We know where I am Ziggy. That's two of us, right?" Peter then just began to chuckle and shake his head as if Ziggy was the confused one.

Ziggy laughed along with Peter, as he looked around for his cell phone. "How about I call the house, just to make sure someone else knows where you are?" he asked. "Then we can get back to talking about the garden."

Peter didn't seem to have a problem with that, so Ziggy called Marcia. She sounded a little frantic when she answered the phone. "I can't talk right now, Ziggy," she said. "We've got to find Peter. He's been wandering off lately and I've got Delilah and Bill out walking and scouring the neighborhood for him. I'm just about to jump in the car and try to track him down. Audrey is going to stay here and let us know if he comes back on his own. I'm a little frantic Ziggy. I have to go."

"Wait Marcia, don't hang up," Ziggy shouted into the phone. Then he lowered his voice. "Peter is here with me. I'm not sure how he got here. He says he thinks he took a cab. But he's fine."

"Oh, thank God," said Marcia. "I'll let everyone up here know and then I'll be right down. You're sure he's not hurt or anything?"

"Not to worry," Ziggy tried to reassure her. "He's perfectly OK."

"Well, he's not perfectly OK, but I'm glad he's safe," said Marcia. "I'll see you soon. And Ziggy? Keep an eye on him."

Ziggy hung up and looked at his long-time friend. They were right there together, but he felt as if Peter was lost and it made Ziggy feel a little lost as well.

CHAPTER THIRTY

"Wow, that was fun," said Al, settling in on Ziggy's loveseat. "I don't even think I'll need dinner tonight."

"Yeah, you were hitting those free samples pretty hard," agreed Ziggy. "Costco sure has the business though. I have to say I never saw so many different kinds of things in one store. It's even better than IKEA or Walmart."

Marcia and Delilah were spending the day at the senior center, cooking up lunch and helping out with the bridge tournament that was going on there. It was Audrey's turn to listen to Peter about garden plans, so Bill suggested that Ziggy and Al join him on a shopping trip to Costco. The trio had made a day of it. After they 'sampled' their way through the giant store and had picked up everything on their list, they decided to stop by a local bar on the way back. After a few beverages and a few games of pool, Bill finally dropped Al and Ziggy off with their share of the Costco haul.

"Well, it was nice to get out, but it's also nice to just stay home for a while," said Al uncharacteristically. He was usually the one that always wanted to be on the go. "Jenny wants me to take the train up to Seattle for a few days. My 14-year-old grandson has a big soccer tournament this coming weekend and she says he really wants me there to watch and cheer him on. Guess he sort of looks up to me, although God knows why. I haven't always set such a shining example," he grinned. "But I'm just not sure I'm up for it."

"That sounds like a good time to me," said Ziggy. "Your family is great, and you don't want to disappoint your grandson. Besides that, you'd be able to squeeze in a visit with Emily as long as you're up there."

"Well, about that," stammered Al. "I may cool the women thing for a while."

Ziggy almost dropped the joint he was rolling when he heard Al say that. "I think my hearing is going," he said. "I could have sworn I just heard 'Al the Man' swear off women!"

Al took a long drag on the joint, coughed a little and then said, "Well, Ziggy old pal, you know when Mona was up here for Bill and Audrey's wedding? And she and I got together the night before she flew back to San Francisco? Damnit, it turns out that Al was not 'Al the Man' that night if you know what I mean."

"Oh, is that all?" said Ziggy. "I hate to break it to you Al, but at our age, that just happens sometimes. Best hope is that you have a partner that understands and then move on. It just happens."

"But it's never happened to me!" protested Al. "And truth to tell, I'm afraid to try it again for a while. What if I'm all used up? It's my identity Ziggy, and I just don't want to risk it happening again with Emily or any other woman for that matter. It's really bringing me down."

"Well if you're really worried about it, there are pills for that sort of thing," suggested Ziggy. "Maybe you should talk to Marcia about it."

"Oh geez Ziggy, I couldn't do that," said Al. "Marcia? That'd be like telling my sister what's wrong with me," he added with a sigh.

"There's nothing wrong with you Al, except maybe thinking you're some kind of superman senior citizen. It's an age thing, Al, get over it. I suggest you head up to Seattle for the soccer tournament and then maybe try a little post game action with Emily. It will either happen or it won't, but you giving up on women is not the answer. Probably not even possible, anyway," Ziggy finished with a smile.

Al thought about it for a while and then said, "Maybe you're right. In fact, I think I'll head home right now and make a few phone calls. I'll plan to leave for Seattle on Thursday. Thanks for the pep talk, Zig," Al said as he headed for the door.

Ziggy was feeling pretty good about the advice he gave Al until Al poked his head back inside for one final comment.

"Oh, by the way Ziggy, the big garden clearing party is next weekend up at the house. Have fun, I'll be thinking of you guys."

CHAPTER THIRTY-ONE

"I'll tell you, he may have some problems, but he sure can work," said Stu to Ziggy as they took a quick break from the yard work. "I don't know how he keeps going, I'm bushed already."

"Take it easy Stu," Ziggy advised. "No need to wear yourself out cause I'm sure we'll be having more of these work days as long as gardening season and Peter's enthusiasm continues."

"Hey you buttheads, let's get moving!" yelled Peter, shaking his shovel at them. "I want to get this all cleared and level today so the topsoil can come in tomorrow."

Ziggy and Stu sighed and stood up just as Delilah came over to take her break. "You guys going back to it? I tell you, that brother of mine is a task master, but it's nice to see him so engaged and focused."

"A little too focused for me," said Marcia as she and Audrey came over to join the group. "I'm taking a nice long break, no matter what that husband of mine says."

Stu and Ziggy headed out to the garden plot to join Bill, Chuck and Peter. "That sneaky Al sure timed his Seattle visit right," said Bill, wiping his brow.

"Well, the tournament was this weekend," said Ziggy, trying to defend his pal. "But he did say he'd be thinking of us."

As they were talking, Moon and Turtle drove up, loaded with sandwiches from the deli. "Refreshments for the weary," they said. "We already ate, so we can work while you guys eat."

Everyone but Peter welcomed the break and they headed back to where the others were sitting. As they were walking, Stu stumbled and fell to the ground.

"Are you OK, Stu?" asked Bill.

"I'm not sure," said Stu. "I really don't feel so well."

Audrey rushed up to see what she could do. Bill and Chuck helped Stu to his feet and guided him to a lawn chair. Marcia ran to the house to get her medical bag. When she returned, she immediately started to check Stu's blood pressure and pulse.

"Not so good, Stu," Marcia said. "Your color is terrible. I'm thinking we should take you to the emergency room right now, just to see what's up."

"I'm going too," said Audrey as she sat next to her little brother.

Marcia pulled the car around and they helped Stu to his feet and to the car.

"Let us know how things go," Chuck said. "And you take care, old man," he said to his brother.

Stu smiled and nodded weakly, and the trio was off to the hospital. Everyone sort of just stood around for a while and then started in on their sandwiches, but no one had much of an appetite any more. Even Peter, Moon and Turtle stopped working and joined the group, with no one saying much.

Finally, Delilah spoke up. "Hey folks, he's going to be all right. He's in good hands and if I know my sister, she'll demand proper attention to him once they're at the ER."

"The waiting is the hardest part," said Chuck and everyone nodded in agreement.

"Well, I know what would make the waiting go faster," said Peter. "Getting back to work!"

No one could really argue with that, so they all got up and wandered back to the garden area. After almost an hour, Delilah's phone rang and they stopped to find out what was going on. She spoke on the phone for a few minutes and then reported to the group.

"Well, it looks like the band will be short a bongo player for a while, but Marcia says it looks like Stu is out of danger. The doctors want to keep him overnight for observation and do a few more tests, but his vital signs are stable for now. She said she and Audrey are going to see that he is settled in his room, and then they would be home, probably in an hour or so."

Everyone heaved a sigh of relief. "I say we pack up for the day and head inside to wait for the girls," suggested Ziggy. Everyone but Peter heartily agreed, but he eventually decided that even his workday was done.

After they all got themselves a beverage, Moon spoke up and said that her cousin had the same experience as Stu, and he was just fine. Just had to watch his diet and get regular checkups. Most everyone knew of someone with a similar experience and tried to share some positive outcomes to settle their nerves. Ziggy stayed silent, just nursed his beer and closed his eyes to think.

CHAPTER THIRTY-TWO

O nce I abandoned Carrie and the life I thought I wanted, I went back
to San Francisco. My happy, carefree college days were spent there, so I
thought it would be a good choice. I soon discovered that landing in a new
city and looking for a new life, was not going to be a walk in the park. Just
up and leaving my job in San Diego with no two-week notice, had created a
problem for me when I started job hunting in my new residence city of choice.
I had savings, but my temporary rental was going to use that up pretty fast,
so I started to feel a little desperate and depressed. I decided to get serious…I
went to a bar. I got pretty serious about drinking and being desperate and
depressed and feeling sorry for myself and stayed that kind of 'serious' for quite
awhile. Then one day I saw the light — Tom Light.

I'd seen Tom at my favorite bar pretty regularly, but we finally ended
up on adjoining stools one evening just before dinnertime. We talked about
everything under the sun. Turns out he had been working at a small engineering firm for the past 40 years, and he was looking forward to retirement.
He figured he had no more than 10 years of energy left to devote to working.
I put his age at about 60, so I encouraged him to find his dream retirement
scenario, and just head for that goal. Probably should have set up my own
'dream scenario' years ago, I thought to myself.

Tom had been married and divorced three times, and although we
didn't have that in common, we discovered we had a lot of life similarities.
We had enough similarities and enough beer that we decided to continue
our discussion over dinner at a place we both liked and that was walking
distance from the bar.

After a generous dinner of spaghetti, meatballs and garlic bread, Tom leaned back and closed his eyes. I never even thought that he might be falling asleep on me. I just knew that he used the same method to think as I had for so many years.

"You know, Zeke," he began. "I think there may be a spot for you at our firm. It's not going to pay you the kind of money you were making in San Diego. You'd be starting at the bottom again, but I think you'd be a good fit. I have always thought I was a good judge of character, and I certainly like you, you character," he laughed. He pulled out a cigar and proceeded to light it up and continued. "How about I put in a good word for you, you stop by the place next Monday, and we'll see where it goes?"

I tried not to look too excited, but this seemed like an answer from heaven. And I liked Tom, too, so it seemed like something that might work. "Well, I'd be grateful for any recommendation you could give me," I said. "I'm beginning to get a little worried about my finances, my future, my life."

"Then we'll see you Monday," Tom said in the middle of coughing and puffing. He gave me his phone number and the address of the company, and I bid him goodnight. I left him there, smoking and ordering a snifter of brandy, and said I'd see him soon.

Monday morning, I presented myself at the address he gave me. The name over the office read "Light Engineering and Construction". I was totally surprised. My barfly friend owned the damn company and had agreed to give me a chance.

Turns out he gave me a lot more than that. Not only did I get the job, but he also took me under his wing and really mentored me in ways that I still can't believe. I learned more about my chosen profession, but I also learned a lot about life, aging, dreams… and despair. No one since Paula had taken the time to really listen to Zeke, and to really care. He was my boss, but more than that, he was my friend. I paid him back with friendship, respect and hard work. Things really started looking up for my life in San Francisco. I was able to rent a small condo near the office and I was working and playing with Tom Light. Eight years went by and I finally felt I had found 'my place'. So, it was with tremendous alarm that I walked into the office one morning and everyone was just standing around the door to Tom's office, not looking happy.

"What's going on?" I asked. "Where's Tom?"

Tom was in the hospital after suffering a massive heart attack. He was in intensive care and according to his secretary, there wasn't a whole lot of hope for his survival. She told me if I wanted to see him, I should do it soon.

That's how I found myself back at a strange hospital with nothing but fear and questions. The ICU nurse told me that I was allowed five minutes with him. I tried to pull myself together and went to his bedside. He looked terrible, but still had the familiar twinkle in his eyes when he saw me.

"Zeke, thanks for coming," he said weakly. "I guess my smoking and drinking and unhealthy eating habits have caught up with me. But as we've talked about, life has been a path that I've taken on eagerly and in my own way. Wherever it leads me now will still be an adventure. I'm at peace, really."

I took his hand and mumbled some words, but my heart was breaking. He had been the closest thing to a father for me. This was one time I couldn't run from it; I was suffering.

"But the story isn't over," continued Tom. "There's more to the story, remember that." With that, he closed his eyes and the nurse ushered me out of the room.

Tom died two hours later. His death seemed more like a beginning than an end. I knew I would be doing him a great disservice if I didn't try to keep his thoughts and dreams in my heart, and I hope I have.

"Life is like arriving late for a movie, having to figure out what was going on without bothering everybody with a lot of questions, and then being unexpectedly called away before you find out how it ends."

--Joseph Campbell

CHAPTER THIRTY-THREE

"**I**s Stu all right now?" asked Al as he, Ziggy and Delilah sat up on Al's deck. "Should I go down and see him? Geez, I'm no good with this stuff."

"Relax Al," said Delilah. "Stu will be fine as long as he follows doctor's orders. He has to pay more attention to exercise and a healthy diet. You know the routine. It's what we all should be doing, but usually don't. Marcia got him set up with one of those Life Alert buttons that he wears around his neck, so if he's alone and has a fall again or is in trouble, it will alert the medics."

"How are Chuck and Audrey handling all this?" Al asked. "They must be pretty shook up."

"We've had a few days to process it and talk to the doctors and to Marcia," said Ziggy. "The main thing we can do is give Stu our support, but not treat him like an invalid. We just play it as it goes, sort of like we do with Peter."

"Boy, I could use something stronger than my Sprite for this one," said Al. "How about we roll a joint?"

"Not for me guys," said Delilah. "I'm heading next door for band practice. We're trying to work on stuff that doesn't need the bongos for now. Stu is not quite ready to get back to rocking it out with us."

"I'll be over in a few minutes," said Al. "I've got some great ideas for the band. My grandkids kind of helped me out, if you can believe it. Randy and Gracie really are great kids."

Delilah said her goodbyes and headed over to Moon and Turtle's place.

"Well, I know how your weekend went," said Al. "Gotta say, mine went a whole lot better. My grandson's team won the overall tournament, it didn't rain, and my daughter cooked up some delicious meals while I was there. She's doing a good job and Duane is a good son-in-law and father. Wish I could take more credit for it, but I at least get to reap the rewards."

"And did you see Emily?" asked Ziggy carefully. "Did you get to spend any time with her?"

"I know what you're getting at, my man," smiled Al. "Emily and 'Al the Man' got along just fine. I was sort of prepared for the worst, but I guess life is still full of surprises for me."

"Glad to hear it, Al," said Ziggy. "But just remember what I told you. At our age, it's not always a sure bet."

Al just rolled his eyes and dismissed Ziggy's warning with a wave of his hand. "Sorry I missed the gardening party," said Al. "But it sounds like there was plenty of other stuff to keep you guys busy, with Stu and all."

"We actually got quite a bit done on the project. I think Peter was pleased," said Ziggy. "But don't worry, Al, there's another big planting party in a couple of weeks, and you can bet you won't be able to squirm out of that one."

Al just laughed and said he'd better get over to band practice. They could hear the music coming from next door, and they both thought about the missing bongo sound. Ziggy said he'd catch up on a few things at home and then would wander down in an hour or so, to listen to the progress. "Hopefully you guys will have come up with a name for the band by the time I get there," Ziggy said, as Al headed toward Moon and Turtle's.

Ziggy spent a little time at home, just tidying up the place. As he was emptying his trash and recycling, he saw Bill and Audrey coming down the gangplank with a dock cart full of potted flowers and decorative flower pots.

"Hi Ziggy," said Audrey. "We have a surprise for you. We were at Home Depot with Peter this morning getting more gardening supplies, and we decided that you boys might need some beautification around here. I know Delilah was talking about it, and we thought it would be something for Stu to do while he's sort of homebound. And then we couldn't leave out Al or Moon and Turtle."

"We just splurged and got something for everyone," added Bill. "Just make sure you keep them alive. These things don't grow on trees you know," he laughed.

Ziggy thanked the couple and took a couple of plants and pots from them. He knew Delilah would be thrilled and would put the finishing touches on them when she was through with band practice. "I guess spring has come in the form of good friends," he thought with a smile.

"We're headed off to visit Stu for a bit, and then we'll stop by Moon and Turtle's to distribute the rest of our springtime gifts," said Audrey. "This should cheer all of us up a little."

Ziggy thanked them once more and told them to let Stu know that he'd be down in a day or two for a few games of cribbage. He told them he would probably see them at Moon and Turtle's later.

Ziggy set the plants out on his small deck and smiled to himself. It really did cheer the place up and he knew Delilah would fuss over them and make them fit in just perfectly. He decided to have himself a beer and took his time admiring the flowers and the river traffic. Then he headed down the dock toward the music.

"You're just in time, Ziggy!" yelled Al. "We're taking a break and have taken a vote as well. The name of this great little group is, wait for it…'The Eclectic Eccentrics'. What do you think?"

The band grinned at Ziggy and waited to see what his reaction would be. Ziggy tried to look as excited as they seemed to be. It wasn't a bad name, thought Ziggy. He just had to close his eyes to think about it a little more.

Al explained that the idea came to him in Seattle when he was visiting with his grandkids. His 15-year-old granddaughter mentioned that her crowd had decided that our generation wasn't crazy or lame, just eccentric. Then his grandson asked exactly what kind of music the band played, and Al tried to explain that they were pretty diverse in their song choices. Their ages and musical abilities equally limited and expanded their play list.

"I told the kids it was really hard to identify exactly what kind of music we choose to perform," Al said. "My grandson totally understood and said it sounded very eclectic to him. And bingo, the name came to me…'The Eclectic Eccentrics'."

Clapping started over by the doorway as Audrey and Bill arrived and weighed in in the name. "I like it," said Bill. "Has a good ring to it and it certainly nails what you're all about and what direction you guys are going in."

"I think so too," said Turtle. "And Al has some more good news. We've got our first real gig next month. We're going to play for opening day at the Farmer's Market across the bridge in Vancouver."

Ziggy opened his eyes and applauded with everyone else. Al just puffed up his chest a little, and smiled.

"But there's lots of work to be done before that," admonished Delilah.

"Well, sure," said Al. "We've got to figure out what we're going to wear and make up a banner and some posters and start spreading the word. Lots of work to do."

"Actually," Delilah said with a smile. "I was referring to our music. We're entertaining enough for the senior center and our close friends, but we've really got to polish up our act before we start expecting people we don't know to want to listen to us."

Everyone agreed on both Al's and Delilah's points, and the band decided to set up practices and meetings three times a week until the performance.

"It's a good thing we all get along," said Turtle. "Looks like we're going to be seeing a lot of each other."

CHAPTER THIRTY-FOUR

"We're sure not seeing much of each other lately, with all this band practice," complained Ziggy. "And now you tell me you're going to New York for two weeks!"

"I know, I know," said Delilah. "But my cousin is finally getting married. I promised her years ago that I would be her maid of honor when it finally happened.

And now it's going to happen. As soon as we finish our performance at the Farmer's Market, I'm heading out to Manhattan for a couple of weeks. She's paying for the hotel and the airfare so there is no way I can beg off. And Ziggy, I really don't want to beg off. I kind of miss New York, and it'll be fun to touch base with some old friends and some relatives I haven't seen since dad died and we moved."

"I understand all that," said Ziggy. "But I'm going to miss you and so will everyone else. You know, for us all being retired, it sure seems to me that our days are as full and busy as when we were all working. Except now we don't get paid."

"About that, you haven't heard the latest," said Delilah. "Marcia has gotten all worked up after Stu's heart episode, and she wants us all to get complete physicals!"

"You're kidding me," said Ziggy. "Other than my teeth, I've got no problems that need looking into. What's her deal?"

"She's just looking out for all of us, Ziggy," said Delilah. "After all, we get a free physical each year through Medicare. Even me. As you know,

I just got into the 'Medicare Club' with everyone else, so if it's not going to cost us, why not?"

"Oh D, it always costs," protested Ziggy. "You know that whenever you go to the doctor, they find something wrong, something that needs medication, or further extensive and expensive probing. It's just the way it goes. And besides that, what if they find something really wrong? I'm not sure I'd want to know. It's a little frightening at my age."

"You can try to fight her on this one if you want. But you know our Marcia. She usually gets her way," said Delilah as she prepared to head to band practice.

"Yeah, just like someone else I know," Ziggy agreed with a smile.

"I'm off," said Delilah, giving Ziggy a kiss. "I've got a little something for you to occupy yourself while I'm at practice. We finally put together our play list for next weekend at the Farmer's Market. See what you think."

ECLECTIC ECCENTRICS PLAY LIST

VANCOUVER FARMER'S MARKET APRIL 2018

Run Around Sue (Dion)

Love Potion #9 (The Clovers/The Searchers)

House of the Rising Sun (Animals)

Me and Bobby McGee (Janis Joplin)

Sitting on the Dock of the Bay (Otis Redding)

Wild Thing (The Troggs)

Down on the Corner (Creedence Clearwater Revival)

Twist and Shout (Beatles)

CHAPTER THIRTY-FIVE

"**I** think we're ready for the gig this Saturday," said Al as he stepped onto Ziggy's houseboat. "The Facebook page has been up and running for a couple of weeks, and we're already getting some good comments on it."

Ziggy was truly amazed at how excited everyone was about this band thing. He mainly thought of it as a distraction for some bored senior citizens, and he had not been very keen about all the time Delilah was spending on it. He knew she enjoyed it, but now that he had committed and taken the leap into coupledom, he really wanted to spend more time with her.

"Al's taken care of the PR stuff really well," laughed Delilah. "He's got high school yearbook pictures of all of us and the tag line teaser: 'Eclectic Eccentrics, the most famous band you've never heard.' It's actually quite clever. Good job, Al."

"Thanks D," said Al. "The t-shirts are at the printer as is the banner, and we've got our transportation all worked out. Everyone has been helping out and it's really coming together."

They all reflected on how well things were working out with this 'web of social security' as Peter had named it. The Senior Center was going to get a bus out to the market and Bill talked some of his VFW buddies into coming out for the event. The musicians felt more comfortable knowing there would be some friendly faces in the audience.

"Well, I've been in on the recent band practices and you sound good. It's much better, too, now that Stu is back," said Ziggy. He knew Marcia was monitoring Stu's activity level and that he was taking it easier, but it was obvious that Stu was happy to be able to participate in the performance.

"Speaking of band practice," Delilah said. "I've got to get going. We're going to do our entire play list today at the Senior Center. See you later."

After Delilah left, Al stretched out on the loveseat and gave a long sigh. "Oh, Ziggy my man, this managing business is tiring me out. I haven't been sleeping very well, just anxious, I guess. But I'm kind of glad that Marcia has my physical appointment scheduled for this month. It's just a good idea to get me checked out and see if I need some Geritol or something. Remember Geritol? That old 'tired blood' cure? That's probably what I've got, tired blood."

Ziggy smiled at his friend. Al had always been a bit of a worrier. He acted so self-assured on the outside, but Ziggy knew better. If Al wasn't keeping himself busy enough, he worried that he was slowing down. If he was too busy, then he worried something was wrong with him. So it was now the time to drop a little reality into Al's soup.

"I hate to keep singing the same old tune Al, but I think you need to accept that you're just getting older," said Ziggy. "We all are. I mean, we're not over the hill yet, but we're definitely past the peak, if you know what I mean. We've got a pretty good thing going around here, so you just need to accept and enjoy."

"You're right Ziggy," admitted Al. "But it still bothers me, you know?"

"I know," said Ziggy. "I know."

CHAPTER THIRTY-SIX

"**I** know it's early for you Ziggy, but I wanted to talk with you before I head out to Long Island, and then I'm going to the theatre and dinner after that," said Delilah. The three-hour time difference was confusing for Ziggy, but he was glad to be able to talk to her at any time of day. She had been gone for ten days and there were still five more days until she'd be back in Portland.

"Sounds like you're keeping the midnight oil burning," said Ziggy. "After all the wedding preparations and festivities, I would think you'd be tired out."

"Oh, I am, I am," laughed Delilah. "But it's hard to pass up all the fun stuff going on in this city. I know I'll be ready for a good long rest when I get back home."

Ziggy then let her know that she may not get as much rest as she hoped for, since Al had been busy booking the band for two more dates. Bill had gotten the Eclectic Eccentrics a gig at the VFW's Birthday Bash at the end of May and then the Vancouver Farmer's Market wanted them back for a summer solstice celebration in June. He tried to catch her up on the happenings of the last week or so.

"Well, Al finally had his physical and found out his lethargy was indeed 'tired blood,' as he called it," said Ziggy. "He has to take iron pills now and eat more foods rich in iron. Then, of course, he has to go back and get checked in a month to see if he's improved. I told you these 'free' Medicare checkups always result in more things to check. It's a racket."

"I still wish you'd get a checkup Ziggy," said Delilah. "You've been dragging your feet on that, according to Marcia. I have my appointment to look forward to when I get back, as well."

Ziggy did not want to get into a big discussion about that, so he quickly changed the subject. "We did have a bit of a scare down here a couple of days ago," Ziggy said. "Al and I were sitting up on his deck and suddenly there were flashing lights in the parking lot and the EMT wagon unloaded two guys who came rushing down the gangplank. Turns out they were headed for Chuck and Stu's place."

"Oh, my gosh," said Delilah. "Is everything alright?"

"Yeah," Ziggy said with a little chuckle. "Turns out Stu was taking a nap while Chuck was out and Spot the cat jumped right on his medic alert button. It gave us a scare at first and caused quite a commotion down here in the community, but thankfully it was a false alarm."

"What did Marcia say about it?" asked Delilah.

"She told Stu to make sure the cat was in the other room when he was sleeping, but mostly she felt pretty good about the whole system working and all," laughed Ziggy.

They talked for a few minutes longer and then Delilah had to go. She admitted that she was having fun, but was missing everyone, especially him. She reminded him to tend to the flowers on the deck and teased him about the mess she might find when she got back. She also had a puzzle for him to think about until she got home. She'd gotten together with some old friends from boarding school and they posed the question to everyone: 'Knowing what you do now, what advice would you give your 30-year old self?'

Ziggy promised he'd think about that one. "I miss you, D," he said. "I know I've got Al and the other folks, but you're my best friend."

CHAPTER THIRTY-SEVEN

"You know you're my best friend," said Al to Ziggy one afternoon as he was doing some work on the siding of Ziggy's houseboat. "Of course, I don't have many friends really, but I was up talking with Peter the other day and he started talking about all these friends I never heard of. At first I thought they were friends he'd made in New York, but he made it sound like they were friends he's made since he's been out here in Portland. I don't get it Ziggy, where does he meet them?"

Ziggy agreed that it was a little strange, but also knew that Peter had been acting a little strange lately so it might all be in his head. He would try to remember to ask Marcia about it. "So how is the garden coming?" he asked as he handed Al some more nails. "I haven't been up there in a while." They had all spent many hours preparing the garden plot and helping Peter plant most of the seeds and starts, but Ziggy found it frustrating to then have to wait around for the weather to cooperate so the plants could grow.

"It's looking pretty good," said Al, as he finished up his project. "You should go up there and check out how it's doing. And maybe you can figure out where Peter is finding all these new friends when he hardly ever leaves the house except to come down here."

"Yeah, let's plan on that after Delilah gets back from New York," said Ziggy. "Thanks for patching up the place," he said as he handed Al a Sprite. Ziggy knew he was going to have to lay out some real money soon to replace some log floats under the houseboat. It was sort of a process and they figured he could stay up at Delilah's apartment for a few days while the project was going on. He had to wait for the weather to cooperate on that one, as well.

Al suggested playing some cribbage for a bit before he took his pre-work nap. Ziggy thought that was fine and said that he wanted to take a little nap too. Delilah was finally coming home in a few hours and he wanted to wait up for her late flight. It seemed like a long time to him, even though it'd only been two weeks. She had become such a big part of his life and he had really missed her. Hell, he even missed her bossiness about things.

"I'm thinking about flying down to San Francisco," said Al. "Maybe leave after our gig at the VFW." Ziggy knew that Al was anxious to prove he was still 'Al the Man' with Mona. "Should be a lot of fun visiting some old haunts seeing how the place has changed."

Ziggy could see Al's energy was starting to return as he talked about getting back to some action. "Oh, San Francisco has definitely changed," said Ziggy. "You won't recognize it. I know I didn't when I first moved back up there from San Diego. But I found a few good spots. I'll write them down for you if you want, although I'm sure Mona is more familiar with stuff these days."

"Do you ever feel like going back?" asked Al. "I mean, you like it up here and all, but do you ever miss working and being a part of things?"

"Sometimes," Ziggy admitted. "I guess I miss most of the old days when I had a little more energy, was a little younger. Maybe I could go back to being in my 30s again."

"Yeah, it would be a hoot to go back to our 30s, knowing what we know now," agreed Al. "Might do things a little differently, might not."

As they put away the cribbage board and cards, Ziggy remembered Delilah's puzzle for him. He'd completely forgotten about it until Al started to bring things up their past. "I guess I'd tell myself not to worry so much, to be freer with things, with myself," Ziggy mused. "I've probably missed out on a lot in life by being such a stodgy stick-in –the-mud. To be old and wise you must first be young and stupid."

"Is that another one of your Campbell quotes?" asked Al.

"Nah," said Ziggy. "I saw it on Facebook."

"Well, it's probably true," Al agreed as he headed out the door and down to his boat. "But look at me. I did a lot of crazy stuff being 'freer'. Now and then I look back and ask myself, 'What did you do?'"

CHAPTER THIRTY-EIGHT

"What did you do?" Ziggy gasped as Delilah was putting on a nightgown to get ready for bed. "Tell me that isn't real!"

Delilah just laughed and said, "What, this itty bitty fishy? It's a little something I picked up in New York. And it is real."

Granted it was small and not in a readily visible place unless she wore a bathing suit, but Ziggy still couldn't believe it. Delilah had gotten herself a tattoo. Not that Ziggy really had anything against tattoos, but he really didn't see the point.

Delilah just chuckled and told Ziggy that a tattoo had been on her 'bucket list' forever and she finally got up the courage – (with a little help from some White Russians) to do it. Ziggy examined the fish tattoo more carefully and agreed that it was a good likeness, but still marveled that she had done it.

"But wasn't it painful?" he asked. "I mean didn't it hurt you?"

"No more than the hangover I had the next day," said Delilah, admitting that there was way too much alcohol involved in her East Coast trip and that she was going to abstain for at least a month.

Ziggy looked worried, thinking she would ask him to join her in her pledge, but she didn't. He thought about all her stories from her trip and wondered how she had the energy. Ziggy was never much of a traveler and rather enjoyed just staying at home or hanging around with one or two friends. Of course, the gang up at Sullivans was always fun, but even then he knew he would rather just be alone… or with Delilah.

"I'm glad you had a good time, D, but it's great to have you home," Ziggy said. "I suppose you'll be heading up to your place tomorrow to unpack and see how things are going up there?"

"Yeah, I've got to check in and see what old Peter has been up to," said Delilah with a yawn. "I'm pretty beat, Ziggy, but we can talk more in the morning after I catch up on the time zone zombie feeling, OK?"

Ziggy gave her a hug as she wandered off to bed and he started turning off lights and locking doors and windows. He sat down on the love seat and rolled a joint to think things over. A tattoo? A bucket list? He'd never made a bucket list and wasn't sure what he would have put on it anyway. He was usually content with the way things were, and if he wasn't, well then, he just removed himself from the situation and started over. That's what he'd done when he moved to Portland, wasn't it?

CHAPTER THIRTY-NINE

Work was getting to be a drag for me. I realized that after Tom died, I lost some of my zest for the job. He had left the company to his sons (one each by two of his three marriages) and they weren't doing a bad job, but it just wasn't the same and I was feeling restless. I was one of the 'old men' in the company then and while I got along with everyone, I still felt like the odd man out in most social situations. I'd been working at Light Engineering for almost 20 years by then, and almost that long at the firm in San Diego before that. Maybe I was just tired of the work.

But I knew I still had some money to save before I could retire from anything, so I just kept plugging away. I knew I was letting Tom down. He advised me, on his deathbed to "Finish the story," but I just didn't know what that story was for me. It puzzled me, it frustrated me, and I felt pretty lost.

I drifted in and out of a few relationships, but nothing lasted for very long. I was either too set in my ways, or just too gun shy of getting involved. And truth be told, the women I tended to date were pretty much in the same situation. Their biological clocks had stopped ticking years ago, and most of them had been married before and had no taste for that, so there were no hurt feelings on either side as we hung out for a while and then stopped hanging out. Safe... but a bit lonely.

I did explore volunteer opportunities for some projects in the city. There were a lot of them to be sure. I ended up at the local Habitat for Humanity. I was no carpenter, but I fancied myself as a decent writer (as you might have figured out from this missive), so I volunteered to work on their quarterly newsletter. It wasn't a hard job and I learned a lot about families and their struggles and their amazing ambitions to make a better life for themselves. I envied that kind of drive. I never had a lot of money, but I was pretty comfortable now and I felt good giving back in some small way.

It was a great crew of volunteers and staff and we socialized quite a bit. One night I 'socialized' a little too much and had a hard time getting myself to work the next day. I couldn't call in sick because there was a big project to finish and I had not been keeping up with my end of it very well.

I dragged myself to work and slinked back to my cubicle. I rushed to get the project done because I honestly felt as if I would throw up any minute and I needed to get out of there and lie down and die. I finished my part of the project in record time, turned it in to my supervisor and told everyone I was taking the rest of the day off - which I did. Then I decided to take another day off, as well.

As I finally made my way back to work, my supervisor was waiting for me at the door. "Zeke," he said. "This is hard to tell you, but there was an unforgivable mistake on your drawings and schematics. Unforgivable, Zeke."

He showed me what I had done and I knew immediately that he was right. My God, it could have been a disaster if he had not caught it in time! What had I done? An apology was just not enough. Apparently, I had made other minor mistakes in the past several months, but my co-workers had caught them and they were quickly corrected. But this one was done in such a rush; I'd bypassed the checks and balances that we were supposed to do and that I should have done. I was ashamed. I headed back to my desk. No more was said to me or by me the rest of the day.

But, I finally knew what I had suspected for a while. I was getting lax, I was not motivated, and I was making mistakes. "Time to hang it up, Zeke," I told myself. I survived until quitting time and was thankful that I had the weekend to try to figure things out.

I tried to put things out of my mind, which I was usually pretty good at. But that dangerous error kept popping back into my head. I had a date *for dinner that Saturday night and thought I should cancel. What kind of company would I be? But I told myself to forget everything and just go out, have a good Chinese dinner and a few drinks and I would be fine.*

Things were fine, actually. My date and I had been seeing each other off and on for the past several months. It was nothing serious, but we got along well and we were having a pleasant meal and conversation. As usual, I managed to overeat and overdrink. We decided to walk around Fisherman's Wharf for an hour or so after dinner, then got into a cab and took ourselves to our separate homes. My worries cropped up again once I was alone. I didn't know what to do. I knew my work was suffering and I was suffering. I thought again about Tom Light and his joy for life. Where was my joy for life? What was I going to do about finding it?

Well, you know what they say about Chinese food: You're hungry again in a few hours. My stomach attested to that old adage fairly quickly, so I made myself a sandwich, got myself a beer and decided to sit in bed and watch a little television with my snack before I conked out and went to sleep. As I proceeded to take off my clothes, I felt something in my pocket. It was the fortune cookie I had grabbed before leaving our table at dinner. I put it on the nightstand with my snack and hopped into bed for a little "Tonight Show". The show was mildly entertaining and I snacked my way through it, trying to avoid thinking about my dilemma. To my relief, it seemed to work! That is, it worked until I decided to open my fortune cookie. And my answer and future were on that little slip of paper: "Find joy in a new endeavor."

CHAPTER FORTY

"Well, I've got to say I've had better Sunday afternoons," said Turtle to the group up on Al's deck. Audrey, Bill, Stu and Chuck had joined Al and Ziggy to hear how things were going with everyone.

Turtle and Moon were relating the story of their involvement with the recent protest that had taken place in downtown Portland. "We've been in plenty of protests in our day, but this one was not only frightening, but very disheartening. And it really made me angry," said Turtle.

"The whole thing makes me angry," agreed Moon. "I know you guys don't really want to talk politics and I think that rule is a good one, but something has got to be done with this yahoo president we have and his crazy followers."

Protests were not unusual in Portland. But the reasons and the results were getting more and more violent. Portland had commonly been seen as a progressive playground, but now it seemed also to be dealing with murderous hate. The latest round on Sunday was between right-wing activists and self-described anti-fascists. Being people of color themselves, Moon and Turtle were unable to contain themselves and decided to get more directly involved.

"The rally was a bunch of right wingnuts and their poisonous speech, which, of course, we had to counter-protest and it got pretty ugly," continued Turtle. "We moved to Portland because of the progressive vibe. But in a city that often sits patiently while marchers walk the streets protesting, how has free speech turned so violent?"

"I'm just so sick and tired of all the hate that has bubbled to the surface," said Moon. "I know it's been there all along with many people all over the country, but the way our administration is going is making it just plain dangerous for everybody."

Ziggy, Al and the rest of the group up on the deck all nodded their heads in…what? Agreement? Sympathy? Helplessness? Probably a mixture of all three and more. Most of them remembered their ardent protests in their past during their college-years youthfulness, when idealistic youth felt they could change the world. Well, the world changed for sure, but it seemed to many of them that it had not necessarily changed for the better.

"At any rate," said Moon. "We were lucky to get out of there before arrests were starting. We're not young anymore and don't need that kind of hassle. And who wants to deal with the cops, anyway?"

It was obvious that Moon and Turtle had seen their share of inequality in their lives. And if they thought leaving southern California and moving to Portland was going to be any better, their Sunday experience let them know they were mistaken. And it was sad.

"I've seen a lot of ups and downs in my life," agreed Al. "I just can't see getting too burned up about it all. It's just the way things go."

"You won't say that when they cut your Medicare and your Social Security," argued

Moon. "But you won't be able to do anything about it, because, 'It's just the way things go'," she finished with a snort.

"I'm sorry you guys went through that," said Audrey. "I'm sorry for all of us that things are coming to this. But I do want to remind you that we have tried to keep politics out of our conversations. Seems none of us are too religious so that hasn't been a problem. Politics and religion are always the things that it's best to steer clear of."

Moon and Turtle seemed somewhat subdued by her cautionary observation, but the rest of the group could tell it was still really getting to them. And who could blame them?

The conversation finally turned to another topic - sort of. Al tried to change the subject by bringing up the successful Eclectic Eccentrics performance at the VFW birthday celebration at the end of May. Bill and Audrey had been attending some VFW functions recently and had even talked Chuck and Stu into joining the local post. Both brothers had served in the Navy, and although they were primarily stationed in Hawaii for most of their tours, they had nothing against telling old war stories with folks at the VFW post. Many of the group had managed to stay out of the military during those frightening times, and most of them had mellowed enough not to find fault with those who had served. But Moon and Turtle had several more things to say about the whole 'defense machine,' as they called it.

"I wasn't sure I'd be comfortable with participating in any event at the VFW," Turtle said. "Never been a big fan of those guys, not then, not now." Ziggy thought that maybe his old friend Ned might agree, but kept that opinion to himself.

"We decided to do it, though," interrupted Moon. "Just like that protest action on Sunday, there has to be something that can get us out of this 'us versus them' mind set.

And we figured there might be something to us mingling with some of the so-called 'enemy' is a step in the right direction. And it turned out great. We met some fine people there. But I still have many problems with the whole military thing in in general."

"This is getting way too heavy for me," said Al. "I'll leave it to the rest of you to solve the world's problems. I'm heading down to Safeway to pick up a few things. You guys can stay here and chew the fat. Just close things up when you leave."

"What's he going to Safeway for?" asked Bill after Al left. "I thought this shopping routine that Jenny worked out for us was going quite well."

"Oh, he probably really doesn't need anything," said Ziggy. "It's just that he's had his eye on Elena, one of the Safeway cashiers. He likes to go down and flirt with her once in a while." Another woman for Al and a much younger one than Al had gone for before, thought Ziggy. He decided to keep that piece of gossip to himself. No need to stir things up any more than they already were.

CHAPTER FORTY-ONE

"This looks great, Peter!" exclaimed Ziggy as he and Al surveyed the giant garden. Ziggy really was impressed. Everything looked so neat. Not a whole lot of action to be seen yet, but there were hints of possibilities throughout the plot of land. He was pretty amazed at what everyone had accomplished, especially Peter.

Peter laughed and started to point out what and where everything was. "I have your favorite over there, Al, spinach," he said, referring to Al's new vegetable of choice for his iron deficiency. "And your corn will start coming up back there by the fence," continued Peter. "And this little section back here in the corner is something most of you will appreciate," he ended with a flourish.

Ziggy and Al both smiled at the pot plants that were just starting to come up out of the ground. "I know a family is only supposed to have four plants at a time, but since we have four families here, I figured I could go a little 'higher', so to speak," explained Peter with a chuckle. "And, I've strategically placed them all between the rows of corn, so they will hardly be visible at all."

Ziggy figured if even only half of Peter's marijuana survived, it could still save them all some serious money in their pot consumption budgets. Al just laughed and laughed and said, "I'm pretty sure this isn't what my Jenny had in mind when she told us to be creative to save money, but it works for me."

The three of them continued to walk along the neatly maintained paths between the rows. Peter explained there would be nothing available yet to sell at the Farmer's Market in two weeks, but that Delilah, Marcia and Audrey were baking up some pies and other goodies to sell at the band's event. "I'm confident that soon we'll have some cool produce to sell," said Peter. They continued discussing the garden until it started sprinkling and they decided to head into the house for a bit of lunch. Bill and Audrey wandered in while they were eating and said they were on their way to Albertsons. They looked over their lists to make sure they were ready.

"Seems our lists of needs and wants changes from week to week now," said Bill. "With everyone watching what they eat and all. Well, almost everyone," he added, looking at Ziggy. Ziggy just kept chewing on his sandwich, ignoring the looks from those who knew he was the last hold-out on getting his medical checkup.

They said goodbye to Bill and Audrey and finished up their lunch. Al suggested some baseball on TV, so the guys went into the living room and sat on the couch. Delilah and Marcia were down helping with lunch at the Senior Center, so the boys were alone and feeling somewhat at loose ends.

The game had just started when Peter commented that some of his other friends were very much into baseball. He claimed that they were really gung-ho about Boston and rarely talked about anything else. As he started talking about these friends, Ziggy and Al looked at each other and Ziggy finally brought up the subject.

"Peter, who are these friends you've been talking about?" Ziggy asked. "Have we met them? Are they neighbors around here or what?"

"No, I don't think you know them," Peter said mysteriously. "I pretty much met them on my own, but I'm developing a pretty good relationship with many of them. Come on and I'll show you."

Ziggy and Al began to think Peter's mind and thoughts were getting more muddled as he now seemed to have imaginary friends who were in the house? They followed Peter into the small alcove that was set up as sort of an office. Peter sat down at the computer and turned it on. In no time, Al and Ziggy met Peter's Facebook friends. He had about 12 of them, most with photos, but who knew if those were the real photos?

Ziggy began to get a little worried. "Does Marcia know about your new friends?" he asked.

"Oh sure," said Peter. "She set a few rules before she taught me how to work this thing. I'm not to give out our address or any personal information, but otherwise I can chat with these folks whenever I feel like it. It's a hoot to read the jokes and look at pictures and all that they post. I usually just look at them and then make a comment to keep the conversation going. It's fun and it passes the time when it's too rainy to be outside or if there's nothing good on TV."

Ziggy and Al both smiled a little and continued to listen to Peter's descriptions of his friends.

Marcia and Delilah came in just as the ballgame was ending. They all decided to have a beer and wait for the grocery delivery to arrive. Ziggy asked the women how things went at the Senior Center.

"Oh, I think they had a lot of fun," said Delilah. "I know we did. And I learned a lot about my newly diagnosed osteoporosis." Delilah had been to the doctor for her checkup and the results of her bone scan had just come in a couple of days ago. "I read a lot and, of course, learned a lot from Marcia here, but it was interesting to talk to some of the folks that had been diagnosed a few years ago. It doesn't sound so scary as long as I keep up with my calcium intake."

"Well, it sounds a little scary to me," said Ziggy. "I'm going to have to keep you from doing so much so you don't hurt any of those fragile bones."

"Oh, that's exactly the wrong thing to do," said Delilah. "I need to exercise as part of my 'program' so that means you will too, Ziggy old boy, since you and I are going to be taking some walks before dinner when the weather isn't too nasty."

Ziggy closed his eyes and waited for the rest of it. He knew it was coming.

"And Ziggy," chimed in Marcia. "You still haven't made an appointment for your check up yet. You're the last one to do it, and you know it's important."

Not fond of being the center of attention, Ziggy just nodded and said he'd think about it. Maybe that would end it for the time being, but he knew it would come up again. As in so many other cases, he tried changing the subject.

"I think I just heard Bill and Audrey come in," he said. "Let's go give them a hand."

CHAPTER FORTY-TWO

"Let me give you a hand, Delilah," said Bill as they were loading the supplies in her car to take down to the docks. "Some of these bags might be a little heavy."

"Yeah," agreed Ziggy. "Spot must be eating too much cat food and therefore, using too much cat litter, as well."

"Maybe so," said Audrey. "But I know she's been good company for my brothers, so it's worth it, if you ask me."

As the group finished loading the purchases into the trunk of Delilah's car, Ziggy and Al went inside to say their goodbyes to Peter and Marcia. They got into the car and Delilah pulled out of the driveway, heading toward the floating homes. She started humming one of the songs the band had been practicing for their big performance at the Farmer's Market.

"Sounds good, Delilah," said Al. "I think we'll be a hit when we perform in a couple of weeks. Emily and Jenny are coming down for it, so we'll have some extra fans in the crowd."

"We haven't seen or heard from Emily lately," said Delilah. "I didn't know if you were still seeing her."

"Oh sure," said Al. "It's just I've been a little busy around here. I've been toying with the idea of asking Elena out soon - someone a little closer to home."

Ziggy and Delilah knew about the Safeway cashier that Al had been flirting with. But only Ziggy knew that Elena was substantially younger than Al – younger than all of them. He thought about Carrie and the age difference between them before he bailed. He figured that just because it didn't work for him, that didn't mean that it couldn't work for Al. And besides that, Al would probably move on to something or someone else after a while. As they loaded up the dock cart, Al and Ziggy discovered another reason the day's deliveries were heavier than usual.

"What the hell!" said Al. "This is crazy. It's different beer! Now, I'm OK with that since I don't drink the stuff, but it's in bottles. What the hell?"

Delilah just smiled. "I'm to blame. I told Bill you wouldn't mind a brand change and a change to bottles for a while. He and some buddies at the VFW have decided to do some beer making and they need bottles. He promised that after they get their 'brewery' going, the taste and cost result will definitely be worth it."

"Well, it better be worth this extra lugging around," said Ziggy. "I suppose they also got the OK from Chuck and Stu, so it looks like we just have to deal with it, Al."

"Thanks a lot for deciding for us Delilah," muttered Al. "Feels like back when I was married. My decisions get made for me."

As they unloaded the groceries at Ziggy's, Delilah let them know of another decision she and Marcia had made for some of the group. "We're going to take part in the Senior Center's 'Grandparents Day' sometime in the fall. It doesn't require much and it should be fun, or at least interesting. Al, you can opt out if you want, since you're grumbling and already have grandkids, but the rest of us should do it for the experience." Al and Ziggy thought about that plan as they continued down their route of deliveries. They visited for a while with Chuck and Stu before Al ambled off to his place and Ziggy and Delilah headed back to the 'Delilah'.

"Lots to think about Ziggy, right?" asked Delilah as they settled in with one of the 'new' beers. "Sorry if you guys think I'm overstepping my bounds, but you know how I am. I have to keep you guys on your toes, open to change."

"I know D," said Ziggy, closing his eyes to think about it. "But it seems to me that it's easier for you to do than for some of the rest of us. It's hard for me, but you haven't steered me wrong so far, so I'll continue to trust you."

Delilah just smiled, finished her beer, and got herself ready to head back to her apartment. "It's a fact, Ziggy," she said. "It's all an adventure."

"The big question is whether you are going to be able to say a hearty yes to your adventure." —Joseph Campbell

CHAPTER FORTY-THREE

"What an adventure!" exclaimed Al. The market today was awesome and the band sounded fantastic. We even made some decent money in tips!"

"And the ladies' baked goods sold out in the first two hours," added Bill. "It was fun working at the sales stall with the *Eclectic Eccentrics* playing in the background."

Everyone was gathered atop Al's floating home, toasting themselves for a job well done. Peter and Marcia had been at the market for a while, but headed home before the crowds got too large. Jenny and Emily had come down just for the day and were heading back to Seattle. But the rest of them were relaxing and enjoying their days' efforts.

Moon and Turtle were enthused at how the band had been accepted and appreciated by the folks at the market. Then, sadly, they kind of brought everyone down with their announcement. "Sorry to say this, folks," Moon began. "But we're moving back to San Diego at the end of the summer when our lease is up here. My mom's having quite a few health problems and it's time we move in with her and help her out."

"She doesn't want to give up the house," added Turtle. "But it's a pretty big place and getting too much for her to handle since Moon's dad passed away. It's a bummer to leave this beautiful place and all you folks, but now you'll have a place to stay if you ever want to visit the California beaches."

Everyone was somewhat stunned by the announcement. Many were wondering if that was the end of the *Eclectic Eccentrics*, their cohesive community, and the future for some of them without offspring to help when the time came.

Al, ever the one to try to turn things upbeat, decided to spring his news. "Speaking of beaches," he began. "Jenny told me today that she and Duane rented a big old place at the beach for a week in August and we're all invited!"

Bill and Audrey asked which beach and how the living arrangement was set up.

"I don't have all the details yet," said Al. "She said it's in Westport, a couple of hours north from here in Washington. Ocean fishing, 18 miles of beach, a little casino and lots of food and watering establishments. The rental house has five bedrooms and there is also a condo complex nearby that they can rent extra rooms if need be. Sounds pretty awesome to me.".

"Sounds great to us," said Moon and Turtle. "It would be a great farewell to this area and a fun time to spend in the sand and surf with good friends. Count us in!"

Bill and Audrey agreed and the rest of them said they'd think about it and wait for Al to give them more details.

So, a sad news day, but also a good news day, thought Ziggy. Just like their lives, lots of ups and downs.

CHAPTER FORTY-FOUR

"Looks like Thursday will be a great day for the party," said Delilah as she and Ziggy cruised around on the river. They had borrowed the neighbor's little speedboat and were idly exploring some of the nooks and crannies that could only be seen from the water.

"This weather has been awesome," she added. "It finally feels like summer."

"Well, it should feel like summer," said Ziggy. "I mean, Thursday is the 4th of July. What are we supposed bring to this shindig anyway?"

"Oh, it's Neil and Gayla's party and you know they want to do all the food. I've got a bunch of chips and dip and we'll make sure there's plenty of beer, so I think we'll be set. Should be a fun time for everyone. You know, even though the Morrisons have an apartment here, we see very little of them. When they do come to Portland, it seems they're busy with their daughter and her family and, of course, the restaurant. It'll be nice to just sit and visit with them."

"Yeah, and it'll be one of the last times we'll be able to party with Moon and Turtle too," said Ziggy. "Of course, we'll have a great time at the beach in August."

"Well," started Delilah as she headed the boat toward their favorite restaurant on the water. "I won't be able to go to the beach with you guys in August. Marcia is taking a much-needed break that week to go down and visit her family in Memphis. I told her I'd take care of things at the house with Peter and all."

As they tied up the boat and headed into the restaurant for a late lunch, Ziggy scratched his head and let out a sigh. He had really been looking forward to a little mini vacation with Delilah.

After they were seated and had placed their order, Ziggy said, "Well, then I guess I won't go to the beach either. What fun would it be without you?"

"Oh Ziggy, you need to go," said Delilah. "You and Al could have a good time together and he'll need someone there as he's dealing with his family and everyone else. It'll do you good to get out a bit. Promise me you'll still go."

"I'll think about it," promised Ziggy. "Meanwhile, I'm gonna dig into this shrimp sandwich. It looks delicious."

While they ate, Delilah asked Ziggy how Paula and Suzanne were doing. Ziggy had heard from Paula recently and learned that Suzanne had been diagnosed with breast cancer. She was beginning chemotherapy in a couple of weeks and they were hoping that one round of treatments would clear it up, since they caught it fairly early. Ziggy said he was keeping in touch with Paula to offer some support.

As they untied the boat for their return trip, Delilah said, "I never met Paula or anyone from those college days of yours, and I hardly had any interaction with her at the reunion. You were taking up all of her time. How close were you guys back then?"

Ziggy had to close his eyes before he responded. "I'd say we were pretty close the first few years," he said. He'd already told Delilah that he and Paula had a 'thing' for a while early on in those college years. "We were both kind of poor misfits in those days," he recalled. "We'd each started college a year later than most of the others and we hadn't done much socializing in high school. We were concentrating on getting the best grades we could because a scholarship was the only hope for either of us."

"Makes me feel a little guilty," said Delilah. "Peter and I had it so easy as far as education goes. But I think maybe I would have taken school more seriously if I'd had to work as hard to get there as you and Paula."

"Yeah, it really did make me appreciate my education," said Ziggy. "And my friendships. So, when things went the way they did with Paula, it really upset me a lot. Until I met you, Paula had been the only other person I shared my feelings and thoughts with," continued Ziggy as they pulled up to the dock of his floating home. "Then she started telling lies and embellishing things I'd confided to her, sometimes I didn't find out until weeks after the fact and it was pretty damaging. I ended up miserable and feeling sorry for myself and then feeling bad because it really wasn't entirely her problem, the drugs and all. But her stealing from me was the last straw, I think."

"Wow Ziggy, do you know what you just did?" asked Delilah. "You actually answered my question without evasion! That's quite a step for you!" she smiled.

"I suppose it is," Ziggy agreed and smiled a little himself.

The couple pulled up to Ziggy's dock and he carefully stepped out of the boat. Paula was going to return it to the neighbor and then head back to her apartment. As Ziggy grabbed a beer and sat at his kitchen table, he hoped that the Paula 'discussion' was over, but he knew that Delilah would continue to poke and prod at his past. He really did want to be honest with her, but he knew that meant being more honest with himself. Not an easy task because he knew he wasn't perfect, or even close.

CHAPTER FORTY-FIVE

It was perfect 4th of July weather and there was quite a group in the back yard. Neil and Gayla had invited the regular gang and then added some folks from the restaurant. All ages were represented, which was a good thing for Al as it turned out.

"Hi all," said Al as he joined the group in the backyard. "I want to introduce you to my friend Elena."

Everyone but Ziggy just kind of stared for a moment. Most of them were somewhat used to Al so they recovered and said their hellos. Al explained that he met Elena at Safeway. "I'd buy a couple of things and flirt with her while she was adding up what I owed," said Al. "And then I'd go back down the aisles and pick up a few more things so I could go through her check-stand again and flirt some more," he laughed. "I finally got up the nerve to ask her out."

Bill was the first to recover. "Speaking of food and drink, Elena. Can I offer you some of my new home brew beer? It's probably got a little more aging to go, but I had to share with everyone. And there are some terrific snacks over there, mostly courtesy of our hosts, who just happen to own one of the best restaurants in Portland."

Elena smiled and took the beer Bill offered. "Al has told me so much about most of you. It's nice to finally meet you," she said.

"Oh my gosh, Ziggy," whispered Delilah to Ziggy. "You told me she was young, but I bet she's not any older than Al's daughter."

Neil and Gayla circulated among the crowd, offering plates of food and Bill kept his home brew going as well. Conversations started up and things got less uncomfortable as folks settled in. Peter had offered his contribution to those who wanted it, a healthy size container of his first crop of pot.

"I've never done any home-grown before," Peter explained. "I hope it's alright." Several folks proclaimed it good, while others said they would pass for the time being. Ziggy started looking around for Neil and Gayla's daughter and family. He finally asked Gayla where they were.

"Well, Ziggy, there's a story to that," started Gayla as she lowered her voice and pulled him aside. "Our daughter and her husband have been going through a rough patch lately. I'm afraid it's likely to end in divorce and that's devastating Neil and me."

Ziggy didn't want to pry, and truthfully didn't want to hear any drama on Independence Day, but he nodded (he hoped) in a wise way. "That's rough, Gayla," he finally said. "I imagine it's difficult when you just have to be on the outside and try not to say much one way or the other."

"You're telling me," said Neil as he joined them. "We're damned if we do and damned if we don't. Not sure what the problem is, but we're trying to be patient and listen to our daughter when she's ready to share."

"Meanwhile, we're determined to enjoy this party and put our personal issues aside for a little while," said Gayla. "And Al's 'date' certainly has distracted us from our problems. That's an interesting situation, even for Al."

"Bill's beer is great," said Elena as she and Al joined them.

Suddenly, a small plane or a giant bug began hovering over the group. "What is that?" they asked in unison.

"It's a drone!" said Turtle, quite excited as he maneuvered some buttons on a controller he held in his hand. "It's the latest thing. What do you think?" The group continued to watch as he maneuvered the flying plane-like thing around the yard. "I'm thinking this will be great fun at the beach next month," Turtle said. They all agreed that it was quite amazing, but a little too technical for most of them.

Elena, Al, Delilah and the Morrisons continued to chat as Ziggy wandered off to the food table to fix himself a plate. He introduced himself to some of the people he hadn't met yet and found a place to sit by Peter and Marcia.

"This looks delicious and I gotta say I'm hungry," said Ziggy. "Probably brought on by your gardening success with that pot."

"Peter's pretty proud of the entire garden and how it's coming along," said Marcia. "Sadly, the one thing that's not growing as fast is the corn," she added as she looked at Peter.

"Yeah, it appears to be a great year for pot but not so much for the corn that was supposed to sort of camouflage the pot," laughed Peter. "But it's all good and I've appreciated all the help with weeds, the bad kind of weeds."

Ziggy laughed, and after cleaning his plate, he closed his eyes to think. He was a little sleepy but knew he'd better snap out of it since Delilah wanted to watch the Fort Vancouver fireworks across the river as soon as it got dark enough. It had been quite a day already, quite a party. He marveled at how well everyone got along and how his life had changed in the past few years. He looked over to where Moon and Turtle were chatting with Bill and Audrey. He'd miss Al's neighbors when they moved back to San Diego at the end of the summer. They'd certainly livened things up down at the docks. And it seemed to get Chuck and Stu more interested in things, as well. All, in all, Ziggy thought things couldn't get much better.

CHAPTER FORTY-SIX

"**S**o, are you all packed, man?" asked Al as he stepped onto Ziggy's floating home. "Are we ready to get this show on the road?" Ziggy looked up from his paperwork and then looked at the clock.

"Al, it's only eight in the morning!" he said. "We don't leave for two more hours."

"I know man, but we want to be sure to be ready when Audrey and Bill pick us up," Al said. "Do you at least know what you're taking? Don't forget rain gear because no matter what the month is, it's always rainy at the beach."

Ziggy laughed at Al, who was almost hopping up and down he was so excited. Truth be told, after dragging his feet at the thought of a week away from Delilah, he was beginning to look forward to getting away to the beach.

"Don't worry, Al," he said, still chuckling. "I've got all my necessities and that includes rain gear. But I haven't even gotten my breakfast yet and I want to get through this pile of mail before we leave for a week. Just settle down OK?"

Al finally grabbed a crossword puzzle book from the kitchen table and sat across from where Ziggy was working. As Ziggy made himself something to eat, Al tried to busy himself with the puzzle, but he was too edgy to concentrate. Instead, he started looking through Ziggy's pile of mail.

"Hey Ziggy, you're getting some of this funeral crap too, huh?" asked Al.

Ziggy nodded as he brought his meal to the table. "I guess it's a sign. They keep suggesting I prepay my funeral expenses and stuff," he said.

"I got one the other day advising me to reserve my space in a wall," laughed Al. "It showed a picture of a whole glassed-in wall with all these urns inside. Like I want to be put up there on view with a bunch of dead people I don't even know."

Ziggy didn't even bother to remind Al that once he got in that wall, he'd be one of those dead people. Sometimes it just seemed easier to let Al rant on and eventually turn to something else. And Al didn't disappoint.

"It's too bad that Chuck and Stu can't make it," said Al, taking a small piece of Ziggy's toast. "Audrey said they just weren't feeling up to it. I think she's a little worried about both of them. Maybe we'll hear more on the trip up to Westport." Al looked at the clock and asked Ziggy if maybe he ought to get his stuff out and ready for them to take up the gangplank.

Ziggy realized he would get no peace if he didn't do as Al suggested. He rinsed his dishes, gathered up his suitcase and a backpack the two letters he planned to mail and they got their bags out onto the dock. As Ziggy locked up his place, Al retrieved a dock cart to wheel their stuff up to the street where Bill and Audrey were going to pick them up.

After they loaded their stuff into Bill's SUV, Al and Ziggy made themselves comfortable in the backseat and they were on their way. There was no shortage of conversation and the trip went smoothly. Al told them that Moon and Turtle left early in the morning and were planning to camp at Twin Harbors State Park. They had decided that they wanted to use their camping equipment once more before they sold it, figuring that they were getting too old to camp like they used to. Jenny and her family would already be at the house they rented, buying groceries and getting things set up. Bill and Audrey were looking forward to the condo that Jenny had rented for them.

"The condo has more space than we need," explained Audrey. "But it was rented when we thought Chuck and Stu would be staying there, too. I'm sorry that they just aren't feeling up to coming. They're really slowing down, and I'm worried about them. In fact, before she left for Memphis, Marcia set up appointments for tours at a couple of assisted living places. Delilah is going to drive and check them out with the boys. It's not crucial yet, but we have to think about it, I guess."

Ziggy closed his eyes to think about that. He wasn't really clear on what assisted living exactly meant, but if it meant help with living, he figured it didn't sound too bad. "Well, Al and I will have our own little wing in this house that Jenny rented so it'll be interesting to see what that's all about," said Ziggy.

"If I know my daughter, she'll try to organize the hell out of everyone," said Al. "I mean, I want to just have some time to wander by myself. I may have to put my foot down."

"Well, be careful with that," advised Bill. "Remember, she and Duane are footing the bill for all of us, so we have to keep the peace and be grateful for this wonderful offer. Hey look, we're only about half an hour out of Westport. There's a winery coming up that offers food as well. How about we stop and get a little snack as we'll still have a while before we eat dinner?"

Everyone agreed, so they pulled into the parking lot and got out to stretch. Al headed for the restrooms and the rest of them entered into a little gift shop. The whole place was pretty awesome and the gardens and grounds were a display of Northwest bounty and original art installations. After everyone made their 'rest stops,' they were seated at their table in the winery's restaurant and looked over the menu. There were all types of wine, and even beer and spirits, and lots of appetizer options for snacking. Bill decided on just water as he was their driver, but the rest of them did some wine tastings, although they were mostly beer drinkers. They ordered an assortment of appetizers that included local seafood and lots of additional goodies, including some interesting desserts. After they'd had their fill, they headed for the house in Westport. Al was excited to see the ocean and all of them were just ready to be out of the car for a while.

It was easy to find the house since the grandkids were out front playing Frisbee. As they pulled in, Jenny and Duane came out and greeted them.

"Welcome to Westport," said Jenny. "Have a seat, have a beer and enjoy the weather. It hasn't rained all day!"

The new arrivals eagerly went for beer and lawn chairs and everyone sat around and caught up on things. Jenny explained that Bill and Audrey's condo was just a block down the road and right on the beach. She handed over the keys and told them how to negotiate the big complex that would be their home away from home for a week. She then took Al and Ziggy into the house and showed them their quarters.

"This is great, Jenny!" exclaimed Ziggy. "Our own little hideout." He and Al chose which room they wanted and put their stuff on the beds. "We even have our own bathroom," he said.

"Yeah, privacy is good," agreed Al. "I like it. Good job."

Jenny gave them some house rules (of course). No pot smoking on the property. Not. At. All. They got the picture and agreed. They knew it was legal in Washington, too, but respected that she was trying to keep control of what went on around the kids. As they went back outside, she explained that Moon and Turtle were going to meet them at the Brew Pub down the street in an hour and they had a large table reserved.

As Bill and Audrey went off to check out their living quarters, Al said he wanted to see the beach before he did anything else. Randy and Gracie offered to walk down to the beach with their grandfather and off they went. Ziggy was content to sit right where he was, and took the time to call Delilah. He already missed her.

When everyone got back from the beach, they cleaned up and headed out for dinner. Moon and Turtle were already there and said they got a great camping spot and were all set up. Bill and Audrey arrived soon after and proclaimed their condo wonderful.

"You guys may like camping," Bill said to Moon and Turtle. "But we prefer 'glamping' in our oceanside condo. Good job Jenny, and we really thank you and Duane for this treat."

They ordered several large pizzas with different toppings to accommodate everyone's preferences and then set to sampling some of the many beers that were on tap. The youngsters found a bank of video games off in one corner, so when everyone had eaten their fill and were talking over their beers, Randy and Gracie went off to play the machines.

"What a day," said Turtle. "We should sleep well tonight, assuming our surfer neighbors don't keep us up all night."

"Knowing you, you'll end up joining them," laughed Al.

"You guys better not party too hard," warned Duane. "Remember we have to be down at the docks bright and early for our salmon fishing trip."

Duane explained that he, Jenny and the kids had booked an ocean fishing trip and Moon and Turtle decided to join them. The charter boat had a couple of last-minute cancellations, so they were able to squeeze in Moon and Turtle.

"I've never been deep sea fishing," admitted Moon. "But I've been out surfing and paddling in pretty rough waves, so I'm hoping I won't get seasick. I'm taking some Dramamine just in case."

"What's on the schedule for tomorrow guys?" asked Al. I wouldn't mind getting back to the beach and maybe exploring a little of downtown Westport."

"I'd like to head for that little casino down the road," said Bill.

"I just want to sit on my balcony with a good book and stare out at that ocean," Audrey added.

"I'm up for anything you guys want," said Ziggy. I really just want to go back home and see Delilah, he thought to himself.

CHAPTER FORTY-SEVEN

"**S**o, did you get to do everything that you wanted to?" asked Delilah as they sat in the Sullivan apartment. Peter had gone up to see Bill and Audrey and then they joined the group.

"Oh, we did everything we wanted and sometimes did things twice," laughed Al. "The weather was great for the first four days and then the rains came. We might not have left for home so early today, but everything looked pretty gray and Bill wanted to be careful on the roads, so we packed it in. It was a pretty rainy trip home until we got about an hour outside of Portland."

"Yeah, Moon and Turtle got pretty well soaked and came back last night," said Peter. "They visited us for a while after they dried out."

"The little casino they had was a hoot," Ziggy said. "Of course, we didn't have much to gamble with, but I suspect any slot machine in the world would take our money. It was fun seeing the little town of Tokeland just south of Westport. We watched folks catching crabs off the dock. And their food was great. In fact, the food overall was so good. The best was the fish feast we had after the folks went deep-sea fishing. We stuffed ourselves. I think Moon and Turtle brought back enough for us to have a re-enactment fish cookout sometime this week," he added.

"Lots of new experiences for sure," said Bill. "We had to stop for gas on the way home and I must have sat in the car for ten minutes before I realized we were still in Washington and had to pump our own gas," he laughed.

"Downtown Westport was fun too," offered Audrey. "Lots of little shops to poke around in at the marina and we brought back a few souvenirs for Chuck and Stu."

"Moon and Turtle told us about their drone attempts," said Delilah. "I guess they discovered that drones and kites don't play well together."

"The beach was the best by far," said Al. "Lots of little out-of-the-way places, good hideaways, if you know what I mean," he smiled. They all smiled back because they knew what he was 'hiding away' from. "But turns out I wasn't the only one 'hiding away'" continued Al. "A couple of days ago, I snuck out for a quick smoke on the beach, and who should I discover in my pot spot but my grandson! Randy was just lighting up a joint and I surprised the hell out of him. Surprised the hell out of me too."

"So, how did you handle that one," asked Delilah. "A little awkward I would imagine."

"You bet it was," said Al. "I mean, the grandkids know I smoke pot. God knows I got caught enough times in their garage. But this was different. I mean, it's legal and all for me, but the kid is underage and somehow it just doesn't seem right. But that would have sounded way too hypocritical for me to lecture him. I suggested that he might want to find a better hiding place, or maybe just give it up for a couple of years. What else could I say?"

"You probably handled it the only way you could," agreed Peter. "I know our parents would have had fits if they knew we were smoking pot back in the day. Of course, it wasn't legal anywhere then. Things have sure changed in so many ways," he added as he wandered out to the back yard.

"Well, I'm glad you all had a good time," said Delilah. "Even you, Ziggy. I know you were sort of on the fence about going, but are you glad you did?"

Ziggy smiled at her and said, "Yeah, I'm glad I went, but I'm glad to be back home. I missed you D." And he moved over to give her a kiss on the cheek.

"Oh, you guys, get a room will ya," chided Al. "Maybe I'll hitch a ride to Safeway with Bill and Audrey and catch up on a little flirting action with Elena. I've been out of practice for a week!"

Bill and Audrey got ready to go buy some supplies and said Al could tag along and they would drop him off at the docks when they delivered to Chuck and Stu and brought them the souvenirs they'd picked up. Ziggy was going to stay with Peter while Delilah went to the airport to pick up Marcia. Everyone said their goodbyes and Ziggy grabbed a drink and went out to the backyard where Peter was doing some weeding. He helped him for a while and then went to sit in one of the lawn chairs and drink his beer. Peter finally joined him.

"So, how did you and Delilah manage this week without all of us bothering you?" Ziggy asked Peter. "I bet you missed us, right?"

Peter looked blank for a moment. Then he looked at Ziggy and said, "Do I know you? What are you doing in my yard?"

Ziggy wasn't sure what to say. He'd seen Peter forget things like names and such, but Peter didn't even seem to know who Ziggy was! He really wasn't sure how to handle the situation.

"It's Ziggy, Peter," he ventured. "Your old buddy from college and now I'm living just down the road at the marina. It's Ziggy, Peter."

Peter continued to stare at Ziggy and finally said, "I don't know you and Marcia says not to have anyone I don't know here if I'm alone. You'd better leave until Marcia comes back. She's been gone for a while but I'm sure she'll be back. You need to go until Marcia comes back."

"Peter, I can't leave until Marcia comes back. Delilah has gone to get her and they should be back here any time now," said Ziggy. "Suppose

I just sit over here and you can go ahead with your gardening and we'll wait until Marcia comes back." Ziggy was feeling a little desperate at that point.

Peter just shook his head, but finally went back to his weeding. Ziggy's mind was reeling. He guessed that Peter's was too. Delilah had told Ziggy that Peter was having his 'spells' more often, but this was the first time Ziggy had seen one. It scared him. His old friend was losing himself right before his eyes, and that meant that Ziggy was losing him, as well. He was so deep in thought that he didn't even notice when Peter came and sat down next to him.

"I used to live in New York," said Peter. "Now I live here. I like it here but I don't know why we left New York. Do you know why we left New York?"

Ziggy tried to be very careful with what he said. "I'm glad you like it here Peter. I do too. I think you moved from New York to here to be near your friends. You have lots of friends here. You have a lot of people who really care about you. That's a good reason, don't you think?"

Peter was quiet for a minute and Ziggy held his breath. "Yes, I do believe that friends are the most important," he finally said. "Otherwise you're all by yourself. I don't much like to be by myself. I like my friends. Would you be my friend?"

"Always and forever Peter," answered Ziggy with tears in his eyes. "Always and forever."

CHAPTER FORTY-EIGHT

"It's amazing," said Marcia. "I can see so much better now and only need my glasses for reading." She had been down to the docks to check on her 'patients' and was visiting with Ziggy and talking about her recent cataract surgery. "Everything is so much clearer, I'm not sure why I put it off as long as I did."

"That's great Marcia. I'm happy for you," said Ziggy. "But how painful was it?" Marcia allowed that it was pretty uncomfortable but the benefits were outweighing the minor hassle. "That's true for most people, Mr. Martin," said Marcia sternly. "If you would only go in for a checkup, I know all of us would feel better."

"But I feel fine already," protested Ziggy. He had been battling his one-track-mind nurse/friend for months now, but was sticking to his guns. "I promise that when I feel bad, then I'll go in for a checkup," he said.

"Well, you know I don't agree with that plan," said Marcia. "We could have lost Stu with that kind of thinking. But it's your choice and I'll stop nagging. For now."

They chatted about things in general and Peter in particular. Marcia explained that Peter was now in a group for dementia patients two afternoons a week. She said he seemed to like it and she trusted the therapists that ran the group. And she did admit that she was enjoying the time off on her own without having to worry about him. "You know, Ziggy," she said as she prepared to leave for Chuck and Stu's, "Peter seems really happy most of the time. He gets confused, but he seems happy. I sort of envy him that carefree attitude. We all seem to dwell too much on our old age, our infirmities, our finances and such. We don't always just take enough time to be happy."

Ziggy nodded in agreement and walked Marcia to the door. She reminded him about Grandparent's Day at the Senior Center coming up and gave him a quick hug goodbye. After Marcia left, Ziggy went back to his work in the kitchen. He was making a special dinner for Delilah and he wanted to have everything just right for the commemoration of their one-year anniversary. It was sort of an arbitrary date he'd picked, but figured this was close enough and it certainly would surprise her. Marcia had brought him a special dessert that he'd ordered from the bakery at Safeway and he was pretty sure he had everything else he needed. He admired the basket of seashells and sand dollars that he had gathered for her in Westport.

It's been more than a year since she came into my life, thought Ziggy. When he'd gotten his job in San Diego, he thought that would be it for his life plans. Then as those plans changed and he moved to San Francisco, he was sure he'd be settled in and if not really happy, then quite content. He'd escaped to Portland to erase all those years behind him and just live out his life in solitude. That was not to be, he thought happily. He remembered his fortune cookie prediction during his dark days in San Francisco: 'Find joy in a new endeavor.'

"Well," he said out loud to himself. "I've certainly done that."

His old friends and new friends alike, particularly Delila, had brought him joy. He realized that Peter was right, even in his foggiest of moments: "I think friends are the most important thing."

Ziggy may not have had a bucket list like Delilah, but he realized that his life was full with things he hadn't known he wanted to have. He had wasted so much time regretting and forgetting; that he'd lost sight of the fact that goodness was all around him. He just had to put himself out there to find it.

As he went to check on the anniversary dinner once more, he vowed he would remember the lessons he learned and treasure the friends he had. Always and forever.

AL'S TURN

Well, I've finally finished reading Ziggy's 'diary' and I gotta say he got most of it right. I can't pretend to know all of his personal feelings and his past recollections, of course. And he may have gotten a little carried away describing me and my antics. But mostly, it's an accurate account.

New experiences and changes are colorfully and thoughtfully described. And the changes continue. Changes at the house are less noticeable. Peter's issues have escalated a bit, but there are still so many heartening glimpses of our "asshole you gotta love." Bill and Audrey continue to work together and with all of us (thank God Bill can still drive).

Marcia is and always has been our 'rock' and keeps us sane.

And, I say this somewhat grudgingly, so has my daughter Jenny and her family. Chuck and Stu moved into one of the assisted living communities outside of Portland and they love it. They even got to bring Spot. The place actually looks pretty cool and since it's on a MAX line, we can get out to see them quite often. Jenny and Duane bought the brothers' place and are using it as a family getaway. I dreaded that at first, but now I've gotten used to it. I see the grandkids more often and it's nice to have them around sometimes to help out with the 'grunt work' and offer their new-generation thoughts, dreams and perspectives. And even my bossy daughter has loosened up a little as she ages.

Neil and Gayla have turned most of the day-to-day supervision of their restaurants over to their grandson, Art, who graduated with a business degree from the University of Washington. They spend more time here in Portland and, after her divorce; their daughter comes around more often, as well.

Delilah seems to have lost some of her 'spunk', but still manages to keep us on our toes and is always up for a new adventure. Thankfully, Suzanne is cancer free. She and Paula were down to celebrate her remission with us.

My love life is still going strong. I see Emily once in a while and I've been down to visit with Mona a few times. Elena and I didn't really last very long. I guess the age difference was a little too much for both of us. But I still see her and flirt with her when I get to Safeway. You just never know.

Moon and Turtle are in California, but keep in touch and visit when they can, as does Ned, who is still in Canada and still trying to persuade us that we have a 'loser' president (No one I know is arguing that point).

And my new neighbors are millennials who are thinking about starting a band. They are planning to call the group Future Ancestors and have asked me to help them get some gigs. I'm up for it.

So, we continue to learn and as Ziggy points out in his journal, 'social security' is not just a check each month. It is a community that embraces all ages and all kinds of people. It is homage to the past with a hopeful look to the future for everyone.

"Follow your bliss and don't be afraid, and doors will open where you didn't know they were going to be." —Joseph Campbell

"We're all working without a net." —Peter Sullivan III

"The story's not over yet." —Tom Bright

"Life's too short." —Zola

"We're all bozos on the bus." —Cheech & Chong

ACKNOWLEDGEMENTS

There are many people I need to acknowledge for helping this book become a reality.

I'd like to globally thank everyone I've ever known who lived through the 1960's to their 60's. Some of my inspirations are no longer living, especially my friend of 60 plus years, Retha. And for those still around? CONGRATULATIONS!!!

Although I never met him, I have to thank Joseph Campbell, philosopher to my generation. He would have been a great co-author and is right up there for inspiration with Timothy Leary, the Rolling Stones and George McGovern.

My editor and friend, Barb Aue of September Song Services has tolerated and guided me through this process. Darcy and the other BookBaby folks have helped me get it all together, even when I thought it was all falling apart.

On to the more personal. My friends and family have kept me going. Thank you to my daughters: Lupine, who has given her valuable perspective and advice; and Cory, who has cheered me on during this journey,

Last but certainly not least, thanks go to Larry, art editor and life partner, and to our border collie, Kona. Larry is responsible for the creative look of the book, and if there are still any typos, blame the dog!

I love and value each of you so much, Always and forever.